Dangerous Love

a Novel

R. J. Wilson

PublishAmerica
Baltimore

First printing

ISBN: 1-4137-2563-5
PUBLISHED BY PUBLISHAMERICA, LLLP
www.publishamerica.com
Baltimore

Printed in the United States of America

*I find more bitter than death
the woman who is a snare,
whose heart is a trap
and whose hands are chains.
The man who pleases God will escape her,
but the sinner she will ensnare.*

Ecclesiastes 7:26

There is a particular allure about bartenders. We're the ones hosting the party. We mix the cocktails and tell the jokes. We buy drinks for whoever we wish and throw out whoever we want. Chicks dig us and we get respect from guys.

It takes a certain personality to tend a bar. I'm not talking about the kind of bartender who works in a four- or five-star restaurant. I'm talking about a bartender who works in a no-star beer-stenching rat's hole. When a fight breaks out, we're the ones who have to break it up.

I was working at McDee's Cocktail Lounge and Bar, a neighborhood hangout for cowboys, bikers, pool players, alcoholics, pot heads, cocaine whores, crack heads, speed freaks, heroin addicts, speed ballers, and hookers. And even though my labeling makes them sound like they're the scum of the earth, most are decent human beings. They just got lost while traveling down the freeways of their respective lives and detoured into McDee's. Eventually they all crash. Some burn. But they all want what you and I and everyone else wants – they want to be loved.

I became a bartender because my screenplay writing career was getting me nowhere. I'd been living in Los Angeles for six years trying to make it in the "biz" with some healthy, legitimate ideas. The veterans say it takes either ten scripts or ten years before a writer can sell something. I had a ways to go. I was employed on enough television commercials, television shows, and motion pictures as a production assistant and grip to make a decent living; however, the jobs were difficult to get and far and few between. I lingered like that long enough to delude myself that someday I would "make it."

A saloon I frequented needed an extra hand on a busy night, so I went behind the bar and helped. One thing led to another and soon I was making more money mixing cocktails and opening beer bottles than I was schlepping light stands and 20Ks.

Eventually, I was able to get a full-time gig at McDee's. It didn't take long to figure out who the cast members were. I followed their body language the way a cameraman frames a shot. I watched whispers to the ear, a nod of the head, a hand-off here, a phone call there. I knew what was what and who was doing what to whom.

Yeah, bartending is a crazy occupation. Customers tell you things they wouldn't tell their best friend. They confide in you, draw you into their confidence, turn you on and give you free drugs. Girls got on their knees and sucked me off in the back liquor room while customers were waiting for refills of their Jack 'n' Cokes.

Bartenders rule.

Then one night I met Jules... and my life went straight to hell.

1

My four day workweek started with the Wednesday night shift. By the time I closed the bar Saturday night I would have mixed five hundred fifty cocktails; poured three hundred eighty draft beers; opened a total of two hundred twenty-six liquor, wine, and beer bottles; rang up one thousand one hundred and sixteen sales; washed a thousand and one glasses; filled the ice bins sixteen times; emptied a total of two hundred twenty-five ashtrays; changed six to eight beer kegs; answered the phone one hundred ninety-two times; stocked one hundred seventy-three bottles of liquor; tossed twenty-two empty beer cases; wiped seven spilled drinks; swept broken glass five times; cracked one hundred seventy-four jokes; broken up two fights; cut off three drunks; and ended each night by having to throw out at least one customer before midnight.

A lot of beer. "Coldest Beer in the Valley" the sign read outdoors on the street side of McDee's Cocktail Lounge and Bar. The rear entrance, from the parking lot, had no signs whatsoever.

Wednesdays were at one time a slow night, but they had been picking up lately since I suggested to Dottie, the owner, that we host pool tournaments. I contacted our Budweiser distributor and arranged the event. Dottie was thrilled with the increase in business and gave me a bonus of forty dollars for the idea. I turned around and gave the money to Bones for a half-gram of cocaine.

Sponsored by Anheuser-Busch banners and signs were hung on the walls promoting the cash prize of fifty dollars. Each player contributed a five dollar entry fee. Budweiser products were discounted. I always tried to start the tournament on time at seven o'clock. I believe the flutter of a butterfly's wings in Costa Rica somehow affects the weather on the other side of the world. Same thing with starting the games on time. All actions compound future actions.

❀   ❀   ❀

The night of my true descent into debauchery was a Wednesday. I remember standing at the cash register ringing up a sale, facing the back bar where a large mirror spanned behind and across the length of glass shelves filled with about two hundred liquor bottles. I noticed the reflection of an attractive woman with long blonde hair, in her mid-twenties, breeze in through the rear door. She was confident in her step. Lagging behind her were two younger longhaired men engaged in conversation. I couldn't tell whether they were with her or not. I didn't recognize any of the three. I finished making change, closed the register's cash drawer, and turned to the bar to complete a sale of two vodka 'n' tonics.

A mist of gray-blue cigarette smoke lingered in the air. The jukebox was blaring out Aerosmith's "Living on the Edge."

Peter, a regular of McDee's, called out for a beer.

I poured Peter's third draft of Miller Lite while I watched the blonde swagger to the end of the bar where Peter was leaning and the *Official Pool Tournament Sponsored by Anheuser-Busch Sign-up Sheet* was lying. She said "Hi" to Peter, kissed him on the left cheek, and playfully pulled on his long black ponytail.

I handed over Peter's beer as he explained to the blonde the procedure for entering the tournament. She picked up a nearby pen and signed her name on the sheet. I watched the body language of the two longhairs to see where they were going.

"They're not playing. I am. And I'll take three Coronas and a shot of Cuervo," blondie said, writing, not looking up. Gold hoop earrings dangled in motion.

The longhairs slid into a red Naugahyde booth against one of the walls surrounding the pool table. I delivered the Coronas with obligatory limes to the blonde, poured the shot, and rang up the sale. Peter and she traded laughter. I felt her eyes on me, and when I turned from the register and approached her with the change she didn't shift her gaze.

"Keep it," she said, indicating the change, and swooped the shot of tequila into her small lip-glossed mouth. She grabbed the three Coronas without saying thank you and turned.

I watched her parade away and imagined stripping off the tight black miniskirt and white silk blouse she was wearing from her perfectly framed five-foot-five-inch body. I would have drank dirty water from the white heeled pumps enhancing bulging calf muscles. And since she was wearing no hosiery it would have been easy to ram myself deep inside her without the shredding of nylon. I wanted her right then and there.

I scanned the sign-up sheet and read her name. I looked up to ask Peter who she was besides "Jules," but he was gone. I watched Jules slide into the booth next to the two longhairs. She looked my way, locking her eyes onto mine. I turned away first to resume bartending duties, mixing drinks, and opening beer bottles—most of which had nothing to do with Anheuser-Busch.

It was another five minutes before I announced the rules, appointed a non-playing, non-partisan judge—who was Peter, and wished all the contestants good luck. The first two players were regulars: Charlene and Bones.

Charlene lost to Bones, which was no surprise to anyone, because Bones was the best pool player in the San Fernando Valley. He had a lot of time on his hands to practice banked cushion shots in between sitting at *his* table, smoking Chesterfields, enjoying his gaggle of girls, and dealing cocaine. His popularity must have had something to do with his trade and generosity because it certainly wasn't his looks. Bones was from the backland bayous of Mississippi. No one knew too much about him except that he had spent most of his life in jails and prisons. His attire was western: cowboy shirt and what must have been his only pair of slim-fitting Wrangler blue jeans. His boots were Tony Lama snakeskins.

The rumor is that Bones "suggested" to Dottie one day that he was going to sell cocaine at McDee's and then handed her five thousand dollars cash. Dottie, the enterprising businesswoman that she was, took the money and looked the other way.

Jules quickly became the center of attention to those margining the pool table. She laughed and didn't sit still. She prattled and flirted with both men and women.

"Why haven't I seen her before?" I asked Peter when the first game was in full swing.

Peter raised his chin, showing off his straggly goatee, and blew a ring of cigarette smoke out of his mouth. "Been at Sibyl."

Sibyl is Sibyl Brand, Los Angeles's County Jail for Women.

"A little convict, eh? What she do?"

Peter looked at me as if I'd find out eventually. "You don't want to know."

"Friend of yours?"

Peter snickered. "Guess you could say that. See her over at Valley Bowl sometimes… hangs out at the bar there… works across the street at the pussy club, Cat's Meow, or she used to."

"Dancer, huh?"

"She's trouble, Mickey, the kind of trouble you don't want," Peter said and gulped his beer.

❀   ❀   ❀

Later, I turned around and there she was.

"Another shot and three beers," she said.

"What's the magic word?"

"Pleeessse…"

I poured the shot. "So, when's your turn at the table?"

"Now."

I reached into the beer cooler and grabbed three Coronas. Jules downed the shot. I took her money.

"Wish me good luck," she said.

"Here," I poured her another tequila, "good luck."

"Why don't you join me?"

I poured myself what she was drinking. We clinked our glasses and used the moment to stare into each other's eyes. Hers were a greenish-blue, but I couldn't really tell because of how low the lighting was at the bar.

"If you win I'll buy you another," I said.

"Then I'll win," she said confidently, grabbing the three beers and giving me a wink. She sashayed back to her table thrusting her hips from side to side sexier than the first time I watched her strut away. She placed the beers down on her table, crossed over to the cue rack hanging on the wall, chose a cue, and spun it like a baton. I'd never seen anyone spin a cue like that before. She looked at me and gave me another wink.

I glanced at her two friends. They both were staring dead-eye directly at me. I wiped the spillage from the shots and turned away.

Jules beat Gary, one of our Vietnam veteran residents, by sinking the eight ball with a two cushion bank shot. Those watching the games cheered and applauded. More and more people were taking notice of Jules.

Peter announced two new players.

Jules and I did another shot together.

Since Jules had won a game in the first round she'd have to wait it out to play another winner in the second round. She had time to kill. I watched her work the room and thought about Dottie's celibacy policy.

Dottie didn't want any of the bartenders to have sex with any of the customers. "Mickey, you're fucking too many girls that come in here," she said, getting to the point one day. Dottie was one not to mince words. I was taking inventory in her cramped office where she kept the liquor stocked. She was accounting, the top of her desk stacked with cash and paperwork.

"What's *too* many?" I asked.

"It's bad for business."

"Does that mean I'm not any good?" I joked.

"Well, I don't know that *yet*," she changed her tone, laughed, and hinted good-naturedly, as if there were a chance for a fifty-seven-year-old-New Jersey-red-hair-Irish-broad like her, my employer, with me.

Holy sexual harassment, I thought.

"All I'm trying to say is," she continued, more seriously, "it doesn't work. When you start going out with them... they come in, sit at the bar, see you talking to another woman, they get jealous, angry at you, turn their friends against you... well, they don't come in any more."

"You lose business," I rationalized.

"I lose business. And it doesn't work for you, either. I'm sure you've figured that out already."

"You're right. I don't like a girl sitting at the bar, who I'm—"

"Flirt," Dottie interrupted, "buy them a drink once in a while. That's okay. You're a good-looking guy, charm them and they'll keep coming back. Believe me."

"That's great, but what about me?"

"Go somewhere else for your thrills."

I had to believe her. Dottie had been in the bar business for over thirty years. I had to believe her.

❀   ❀   ❀

I'd been working two hours straight without a break. I watched Jules and she watched me. There was a lull in the drink ordering activity. Jules was dancing with herself in front of the jukebox. Now was the time. Stevie Ray Vaughn was singing, "I Wanna Be Close to You, Baby."

"Hi," I said.

She fed a dollar bill into the machine and pressed a selection. "Hi."

"Here." I inserted another dollar bill. "Pick a few more."

"Buying me songs, too?"

"Sure, why not?" I punched in the letter and number I had memorized for Rod Stewart's "Infatuation." We both studied the jukebox's titles and artists. There was an awkward silence. I spoke first. "Who're those two guys you walked in with?"

"Friends."

"Which one's your boyfriend?"

"The one in the 'Disco Sucks' T-shirt," she said and pressed an AC/DC selection.

She looked up at me, "How'd you know one of them is my boyfriend?"

"A dish like you without a boyfriend? I don't think so."

Once again she studied the play list. "Why do you care?" she finally asked.

"See who my competition is."

I saw the reflection of a curt smile in the jukebox's glass.

"My name's Mickey by the way. Some people call me Mick. Whatever."

"I know," she said and then took a swig of the Corona she was holding. She smelled like baby powder. "I'm Jules."

We gently shook hands.

"I saw your name on the sign-up sheet," I said and took a drag from my Marlboro. She inhaled deeply from her Newport and spun around. I took another drag from my cigarette but didn't spin.

"Do you always try to steal girls away from their boyfriends at jukeboxes?"

"If I did steal you would I get away with it?"

"I don't know, but you might have to be punished for trying."

I thought about whips and chains and dungeons.

"And be careful what you wish for," she said, reading my mind and then dancing with the jukebox as if I were not even there, invisible. She punched more numbers from the play list. I looked down at her braless breasts and thought about what it would be like to swirl my tongue around her areolas.

"So how long you been working here, Mickey, Mick, whatever?" she asked, not looking up, still concentrating on music selections.

15

"Few months. Haven't seen you before, though. I would've remembered."

"Been away… on a vacation of sorts."

"Nice to have time on your hands."

"*Too* much time."

"You from L.A.?"

"No one's *from* L.A…. from here and there."

"Hey, Mickey, how 'bout some service, man," I heard from the bar area. The extras were getting restless.

"Have to get back to work."

"Short break."

"Maybe we'll talk later."

She stared into my eyes and surrendered a smile, hinting half-truth and half-lie,

"I hope we do."

As if on cue, Santana's "Black Magic Woman" began to pulsate the air. I played the role of bartender again. Jules danced with the jukebox. As I watched her, she reminded me of a black magic woman. I got the feeling she was going to make a devil out of me.

❁ ❁ ❁

During the course of the next few games Jules and I made it an occupation to preoccupy ourselves with eye contact. She slowly approached me at the bar. "Can I buy *you* a shot?" she asked as she pulled out a few green bills from a hidden pocket of her miniskirt. Another button on her blouse had come undone.

"Looks like your blouse is coming apart," I said as I prepared another tequila for her and me. She feigned coyness and put a fifty dollar bill on the bar. I handed her the glass and held mine up fashioning a toast. "Okay, what do we drink to?"

She curled her forefinger three or four times indicating I should move in closer to her. I did and she leaned in and whispered in my ear, "How about we drink to getting to know each other?"

16

I looked down her blouse at her breasts, nipples hard like brand new pencil erasers. "Wouldn't you rather drink to winning the tournament?" I asked her.

"Okay, that too."

"What about the boyfriend?"

"What boyfriend?" she answered, smiling wickedly.

I smiled a little wickedly myself.

"Are we just going to stand here holding these or are you going to let me shove this down my throat?" She said *shove this down my throat* as if we were ready to engage in oral sex.

We clinked our glasses together and the liquid gold was history. I took her money and watched her spin. I laid the change down: forty-two dollars.

"Got a pen?" she asked as she grabbed for a nearby cocktail napkin.

I handed her the pen I always kept tucked away behind my right ear.

"What time you getting off?" she asked as she wrote.

"By the time I close and clean up I'll be out of here around three, why?"

"Be here at three-o-five." She handed me the napkin. It was wet. "Then we'll *really* get to know each other."

I looked down at directions on the napkin. Yeah, okay, it was legible. I tucked it into my jeans pocket next to a hard-on building inside. When I looked up Jules had disappeared. She left me a twenty dollar tip.

Peter, who was standing nearby and witnessed the evening between Jules and me flirting, snickered. "Trouble," I was able to read from his lips.

"I know," I mouthed back.

I interpreted the remark about getting to know me as whimsical innuendo. And again, I couldn't help but look in the direction of her two male friends. I was pleased to see her boyfriend engaged in deep conversation, hoping he and his buddy were discussing a chord change in a song they were probably writing together and not a cosmetic change they were going to compose on my face. I cleared the glasses and headed towards the opposite end of the bar.

Jules wasn't the cue-baton-twirling pool hustler she had been in the first game. Probably too much to drink. Without much care she lost to Bones, sinking the eight ball way before its time.

After she lost there seemed no reason to stay. She corralled her two friends and without fanfare or saying a word or even looking in my direction she pirouetted out the rear door with them in tow.

I watched the three on the security monitor fastened on the wall above and behind the bar, the stationary lens outside perpetually aimed at the rear parking lot. I saw Jules fumble into the passenger seat of a beat-up Toyota Corolla as her "boyfriend" maneuvered himself behind the wheel. Jules gave a wave to the camera, somehow knowing that I was watching her. The exhaust-fumed car sped away reeling up gravel.

❀   ❀   ❀

I handed the winnings of the pool tournament to Bones. Two hours to go before quitting time. I reached inside my pocket and pulled out the napkin with the directions. I was suspicious about the boyfriend. I said, "Fuck it," to myself and threw away the napkin. I'd see her again, another night, another time.

❀   ❀   ❀

Everyone had gone. I was counting cash and adding gross receipts. Charlene sometimes stayed to help me clean. Charlene wasn't much to look at because she was exceedingly fat; but she was fun to be with and a good friend. She kept up with current events like I did and always sat at the end of the bar and read the *Los Angeles Times*. Together we had solved many of the world's problems. And she knew absolutely more than anyone about the gossip that floated around at McDee's.

Charlene was helping me stock beer when the telephone rang for about the forty-seventh time that night. Charlene answered it, "McDee's," and listened. "For you, lover boy," she said and dropped the phone's handset on the back bar.

"You still want me tonight?" I heard a woman's voice say on the other side of the wire.

"Depends. Who is this?"

"Make it three-thirty." It was Jules and she was talking softly as though she didn't want to be heard on her side of the line.

I looked at the Coors Light Silver Bullet clock on the wall and figured I could take my time counting money and cleaning.

"Not any later, I want to get out of here."

"I'll be worth the wait."

"Why are you whispering? Where are you?"

"Shhhh," she warned me as if I was the one sneaking the call, "I'm at my boyfriend's."

Again with the boyfriend.

"My *friend's*," she corrected herself. "Three-thirty," she repeated.

"Maybe this isn't going to work out."

"He's just a *friend*. He's really not my boyfriend. I was just saying that…. playing with you. I'm in his bathroom on the cordless. I'm waiting for *something* for us, for you and me."

"I need directions again."

"Why, what you do, throw them away?"

"I don't know, they're around here somewhere," I lied.

She gave me the directions again and I wrote them down on a piece of register paper. "All right," then I asked, "you sure you want to do this?"

"Does a cat meow?"

Click. Muted silence. No goodbye, see-ya, can't wait to do ya, just click.

Boyfriend.

I glanced at Charlene, who had heard my side of the conversation. She knew already what was going on and what I was up to. I wanted

19

to ask her about Jules; however, I was afraid of the truth Charlene would tell me, so instead I just said, "I'm seeing that girl Jules tonight."

Charlene raised an eyebrow and threw an empty Rolling Rock case on the floor and swept back her long brown hair.

"Oh, yeah?" was all she said. But I knew by the way she threw the empty case on the floor and said "Oh, yeah?" she didn't approve. In some strange way that bothered me.

I made eight hundred fifty-two dollars for the bar that night and a hundred ninety-three in tips for myself. Not bad since Wednesdays before the tournaments we would have grossed only five hundred. At that rate maybe Dottie would give me a break from her celibacy policy.

Okay, so I had been warned about cue-twirling-just-got-out-of-jail-spinning-*he's-just-a-friend*-Jules. I rewound the videotape in my head and played back our flirting, dialogue at the jukebox, her invitation, and the conversation we had on the phone.

I wanted her.

2

I drove my 1991 Mustang convertible, top down, onto Jules's street and found the house. The directions were so easy that if I weren't so stoned and drunk I'd have been able to remember without writing them down. All I had to do was make a right out of the parking lot and make a second right after going underneath the overpass of the San Diego Freeway. Her place was seven houses down on the left. It was a ranch with connecting garage in disrepair. Two cars were parked in the driveway, a dented Datsun and a black BMW 325i with smoked-tinted windows. I parked my Mustang on the street in front of the house and shut off the engine. The house was dark.

I inched along onto the porch littered with rusted lawn chairs and empty cardboard boxes. Curtains were drawn across a picture window. I opened a screen door. It was hanging on one top hinge and almost fell off in my hand. I knocked gently and waited. No answer. I turned around to peer through an angle of the window to see if there was any sign of human motion in the house. The curtains moved slightly and a moment later the door opened two inches. A chain lock was attached from the door to the jamb. I could barely see the form of a person. An eyeball hinted to me that yes, it was human.

"Who is it?" a man's voice asked affably enough.

I answered who I was while wondering who *he* was: boyfriend layover? friend? roommate? The door closed. I heard jingling of the chain drop against the jamb and then the door opened wide. I was greeted warmly. "Hi, come on in, I'm Bill, Jules's roommate," Bill said, offering his hand to shake.

I entered the dimly-lit living room of the house. The only light came from T.J. Hooker on the television set, the sound barely audible. What impressed me immediately were all the other televisions in the room, their black screens silent. Some were still in unopened boxes that read Magnavox, Zenith, and Sony Trinitron. Other brand name electronic consumer goods were lying about in and out of boxes in the cramped room: Panasonic CD players and video cameras, Toshiba radios, a Sanyo VCR, other Sony products.

The floor was cluttered with videocassettes, *Playboy, Hustler,* and *Swank* magazines, Compact Discs by Simply Red, The Smithereens, AC/DC, Black Sabbath, and Mötley Crüe. The dirty walls were covered with paint or wallpaper, I couldn't figure out which. Overfilled ashtrays littered a small beat-up wooden coffee table in front of a tattered couch against the picture window and curtains.

Jules had been renting the house with Bill, who was truly just a roommate and brother of Stephanie, a twenty-two-year-old prostitute working Sepulveda Boulevard two blocks away. In all of my subsequent visits to this house, I met Stephanie only once. At that time she sat in front of Jules's dresser mirror and teased her hair for fifteen minutes without ever shutting up.

Bill posed no threat and seemed like a genuinely nice guy. He had dirty-blonde surfer's hair, long and unkempt. A skinny body not getting enough nourishment. His jeans and T-shirt looked slept-in. He sat down in a ripped and duct-taped brown leather recliner in front of the television as if claiming his territory. "Jules," he whispered loudly, "Mickey's here." Bill's choice of drug was everything, but he particularly liked shooting speed balls, cocaine mixed with heroin.

"I know," I heard from beyond a well-lit entrance into a kitchen. Jules stepped out from the archway dressed as when I first met her except she wasn't wearing her high-heeled pumps. She was delicately holding a long glass test tube at the top by the finger tips of her left hand and circling the tube in such a way as to make a cloudy yellowish liquid at the bottom create its own maelstrom. She was just in the middle of cooking up some cocaine and would I like to come in?

I followed her into the kitchen, stepping over piles of clothes, empty Newport and Marlboro cigarette boxes, scattered Milky Way candy bar wrappers, and haphazardly thrown videocassettes boasting such titles as "Sexual Encounters of the Lustful Kind," "Tammy's Tricks," and "Football Fetish Fantasies."

Jules continued swirling the glass tube and placed the bottom of it an inch above an open flame gas burner on the stove. The blue flickering flame danced, licking the tube. Next to Jules stood two large black dudes dazzled by the chemistry. Both were wearing baggy 501's jeans and drab-colored Pendleton shirts. They both glanced at me. One acknowledged, "Hey." He was wearing a blue L.A. Dodgers baseball cap backwards. The one who didn't acknowledge me had a blue flag hanging out of a left rear pocket. He wore lots of gold: a Turkish rope chain around his neck, Rolex watch and bracelet on his wrists, rings on his fingers, and a gold stud in his left ear lobe. I knew now who owned the BMW.

"Hey," I said back.

They were in the middle of discussing each of their own methods of freebasing cocaine—freeing the benzoylmethylecgonine alkaloid from its hydrochloride salt. The solution at the bottom of the glass tube came alive with the sound of crackle and pop.

I had experimented with a wide variety of mind-altering drugs since the first time I smoked pot at the age of thirteen. That was twenty-one years earlier. I smoked, injected, inhaled, and swallowed everything from barbiturates to amphetamines. Lately I had been heavily into snorting cocaine. It was hard to get away from at the bar. Everyone indulged, including the Geritol crowd. Cocaine helped me through long hours of work and made my life more manageable—so I thought. However, so far, freebasing—smoking crack, or "ready rock" as it is now more commonly known—had never raised its ugly head to seduce me.

Bill, apparently feeling left out, appeared under the archway of the kitchen entrance as everyone was now cramping Jules's own perfected style of cooking.

"Get out!" she yelled at Bill.

Too many cooks do spoil the broth.

He obeyed, muttering, "Fuckings…" under his breath and retreated to the living room to continue watching T.J. Hooker stake out a drug factory.

"Okay! Everybody out of my kitchen!" I realized then how blue her eyes really were. They matched the blue of the gas—as much on fire. "Except you," she said to me. "You can stay."

"That's okay, it's a little crowded in here anyway," I said and turned to reenter the dining room/living room area. "Hey" and the other black dude ignored me. I stood next to where Bill was nervously sitting. I fixed my eyes on the television not paying attention to what was on the screen. I absorbed my new surroundings. The scene was not what I had envisioned driving over there. I thought for sure Jules would be alone. Instead, I pondered being inside a strange house with not one person I knew.

A few moments later Jules walked out of the kitchen. The two black dudes followed her. She held little pieces of American-cheese-colored pebbles cupped in her left hand and a short straight glass pipe blackened at the end in the other hand. She let Bill take his pick at one of the little rocks. She offered me the same but I shook my head. "Suit yourself," she said. The black dudes were the last to be offered. She dropped a nice-sized nugget at the top of her stem, lit a butane lighter, and in the middle of the living room, with T.J. Hooker car-chasing after drug dealers on the television, Jules inhaled deeply and held her breath for ten long seconds. She then exhaled a plume of gray smoke. The odor was faintly metallic. A dazed glint glazed over her eyes. She slowly approached me, stood on her toes, and stuck her tongue into my dry, alcohol- and cigarette-tasting mouth. We swirled our tongues round like small eels squirming inside. She licked what saliva I had remaining from my lips. Bill and the two black dudes didn't pay any attention to us since they themselves were more interested in their own pipes and their own brain diffusions.

After Jules finished sucking what wetness I had left from my mouth, she gave me a mischievous smile and lit her pipe again. Bill fidgeted in his recliner and bit his nails. Hey searched for something in between the love and life lines of his left palm. The other black dude paced. It was stifling hot in the house. All the doors and windows were shut. There was no air conditioning or fan to circulate the stale air.

"I hope you don't mind if I help myself to a glass of water," I said to Jules after she finally exhaled another cloud of smoke from her lungs. She didn't respond to my request in any way whatsoever. I left them all to their respective trances and went into the kitchen.

This time I gave the kitchen a good once over. It was filthy. There was a pile of unwashed dishes in the sink that spilled over on top of the counter. Empty bottles of Heineken, Bacardi, Beefeater, and Hennessy were scattered everywhere. A large black plastic garbage bag filled above and beyond capacity sat propped in the corner barely on its own recognizance. Next to the stove was an open box of Arm & Hammer Natural Baking Soda advertising the words, "A House-Full of Uses!" The empty test tube—which was probably a glass cigar container—laid on its side next to a saucer filled with the same cheese-colored nuggets Jules and the others were now smoking. Blue gas was still burning.

I started opening cabinet doors looking for a clean glass.

Generally, I think opening doors and drawers in someone's house is a rude thing to do. Even though I asked permission, I still felt I was trespassing. I remember one time inviting a girl over to my apartment for the first time. Before she sat down she proceeded to make herself at home by walking around opening doors, closets, cabinets, and drawers. She said she learned a lot about a person by what they had hidden. I didn't think placing my own possessions in closets, cabinets, and drawers in my apartment was hiding. Later, I noticed a hairbrush and a box of Trojan lubricated condoms missing.

I couldn't find a clean drinking glass so I rinsed one out.

Jules burst into the kitchen followed by the two black dudes. Bill followed. There were five of us now crowded in the cramped kitchen. I drank the water and listened to them argue.

"Okay sister, time to pay up," the dude who'd said "Hey" to me said to Jules. Jules gingerly placed down her pipe on the saucer next to the nuggets. She switched off the gas burner.

"I already paid you," Jules said, reaching for a nearby pack of Newports.

"What the fuck you talkin' about?" Dude Number Two said.

"I paid you," she said confidently as she lit a cigarette. She stood her ground, even though she did take a step back.

"You stuck on stupid, girl?" Dude Number Two said.

Bill stood under the archway not saying anything. We shared a glance that was neither here nor there. I supposed that sort of thing went on all the time around there. I stood motionless, sipping my water, minding my own business. I had nothing to say and it would have been uncalled for, for me to do so. I didn't know any of those people. It didn't matter if they were drug addicts, thieves, or murderers, I was a guest in that house and I had to show that respect. I remained silent.

"Them's our rocks," Dude Number Two continued, "You ain't given us our money from the last time, and until you do, them there's ours." He was beginning to get angry.

Jules stood silent, scheming, inhaling her cigarette. Smoke filled the kitchen. The black men stared at Bill menacingly; they towered over Jules but she wasn't intimidated in the least.

Hey shook his head, glanced at the floor, then up at me for some reason. He then turned his attention back to Jules. "We fronted you the last time, bitch, and for the *last* time."

"How much do I owe you?"

"Two forty," Dude Number Two said.

"Take the Trinitron," Jules offered.

"Bitch, we got 'nough televisions, we can't git rid of da ones we got," Dude Number Two answered quickly. He was clearly more pissed-off about this than Hey was.

"Bill, give them the money."

"What?" Bill said with annoyance.

"Give 'em the money."

"I thought *you* had the money."

"I do, it's in my room. Just give them the money now and I'll pay you back later. What's the big fucking deal?"

"The big fucking deal is that's what you said last time and I still haven't seen it."

"You'll get it. Now give them the money."

Bill reached reluctantly into his pocket and came out with a stack of bills. He counted out two hundred forty dollars in twenties, tens, and fives, and handed them over to Hey.

"What's this?" Hey said, referring to all the low denominations.

"It's money," Jules said and blew cigarette smoke into Hey's face.

"Sister, you fuckin' with the wrong people here," Hey said, "give K Dog and me 'nother hit."

For the next twenty minutes Jules, Bill, Hey, and Dude Number Two – who was called K Dog – cooked and smoked more rock. They all re-fell into hypnotic stupors, although Jules and K Dog seemed to have handled their highs more lucidly. Jules offered me another hit and this time I accepted it; however, I don't think I held my breath long enough because I didn't feel any different. Besides, like I said, I was already stoned and drunk when I got there.

❁   ❁   ❁

Jules led me by the hand down the hallway and into her bedroom at the back of the house. The bedroom was large yet cramped due to the queen-sized bed, dresser, bureau, and closet, all overflowing with wardrobe and props: leather, lace, rubber "second skins," what looked like the entire Gianni Versace bondage collection, a score of shoes, one set of handcuffs, and a nine-inch strap-on dildo.

The one chair in the room was covered with more clothes so I sat on the bed. The sheets were black satin.

Jules lit a half-dozen candles, closed the door and locked it. She placed her pipe and rocks down on a broken mirror lying on the top of her dresser next to endless varieties of Estée Lauder, Clinique, Revlon, and Christian Dior cosmetics. She opened a window and turned on a Sanyo CD-radio player. The boom box was scratched, dented, missing knobs, and the FM antenna was broken off at the base. It looked more like a casualty from a previous battle than a music system. The volume was preset to a high decibel level. Apparently it already contained her favorite CD at the time, because she kept playing the same song over and over and over; something about being tangled in a web by some group I have never heard.

Jules dropped a large piece of rock into her pipe, handed it to me, lit it. I inhaled slowly, deeply, and held my breath. Jules then climbed on top of the bed and danced.

Jules was running her hands up her legs at the same time I was beginning to feel a wonderful warm frozen rush to my head. I put another piece of rock in the pipe, but when I inhaled again I felt no more frosted than the first rush. I immediately wanted that rushed feeling again. This is called "chasing the pipe" and why addicts go through so much money searching for that same extreme, rapid initial impact of blood constricting the vessels in the heart and brain. The urge to need and want more is overwhelming. I understood at that moment why a person who smokes crack will do anything for more and will go to abominable lengths to get their fix. This is seduction. This is addiction.

Jules took the pipe away from me. She placed it gently down on the broken mirror, hopped up on the bed again, and continued to dance. I slumped to the floor, and with my back against the wall, I sat mesmerized by her moves. My private dancer. She was wired and danced as though demons were edging her on.

Jules teasingly stripped off her blouse and miniskirt. She was wearing no panties. What looked like an appendix scar was welted across her lower right belly. A small tattoo of a heart with a dagger plunged into it and blood dripping was engraved just above the left cheek of her small but well-proportioned ass.

The high I was experiencing made me incredibly horny. I started sweating and after four or five minutes I couldn't stand just watching her any more. I tackled her down onto the bed. She squirmed, playfully trying to get away from me. I spread her legs and went down on her. She arched her back and moaned. I thought of Peter. Then I fucked her. I eventually pulled out and jerked onto her stomach. She told me later I didn't have to pull out, that she had herself "fixed."

There was a knock on the door. It was Bill and he wanted the money Jules said she had in her room. Jules yelled for him to go away. She started *that song* again which was beginning to grow on me.

❁   ❁   ❁

Before nine a.m., I had spent all of my tip money on cocaine. But I knew I still had fifty dollars in my wallet. (Jules never had any money in her room.) Hey and K Dog were gone, leaving Bill pacing the house nervously. Jules and I had done our last hits, and exhausted by our lust we had fallen asleep.

❁   ❁   ❁

I woke up with a start and jack-knifed out of bed. At first I didn't know where I was. I had a hangover the size of Montana. Jules was nowhere in the room.

I stumbled to the window and pushed a beige torn window shade to the side. It was cloudy outside and raindrops were softly pelting against the rear of the house. I nearly panicked because it looked like it was early evening and I had to be at work at six. Since my hands are always in water washing glasses at the bar, I didn't wear a watch. As I looked around the room searching for the time, my panic intensified. I had a feeling it was very late in the day.

I slipped on my Levis and white T-shirt and then tried to open the door. The door was stuck. With an angry and forceful tug I flung the door open and entered the hallway towards the living room. A bad mood suddenly engulfed me. Jules was sitting alone naked on the floor, in the dark, bent over the cheap wooden table. She was scraping her crack pipe with the end of a straightened-out wire hanger. The late afternoon haze was streaming through a narrow parted vertical slit of the curtains.

"What time is it?" I asked without a more friendlier greeting.

"Look in the kitchen."

I looked at the clock with a blue duck on its face hanging crookedly over the kitchen sink. It was five minutes before six o'clock, exactly when I had to be at work. I needed to get out of there as soon as possible.

"Fuck!" I said to myself. I quickly turned and reentered the living room. "Why didn't you wake me?" I asked Jules.

"Oh, why, was I supposed to?" was her tweaked out response.

At that moment it began to rain more heavily, and I realized that I might not have put the top up on my car. I parted the curtains to see if I had. The only car I saw was the Datsun. My white Mustang was not in the street and nowhere in sight.

"Hey!" Jules cried out, annoyed as if the daylight would have melted her.

"Where's my car!?"

"Bill's got it."

I closed the curtains and glared at Jules. "WhatdoyoumeanBill'sgotit?"

"He went to get something."

"Who said he can take *my* car?"

"Don't worry about it," then she said, "he put the top up," as if that justified it all.

"I've got to get to work. Why couldn't he take the Datsun?"

"It's not running too good, and besides, it's not registered." She then lit the pipe but no smoke came out.

"What the fuck is wrong with you?" I asked clearly.

"What's *your* problem?"

"Oh nothing," I said sarcastically, "I just need to get to my job, but I can't because I don't have my car!"

"Don't yell at me. He'll be right the fuck back."

Jules couldn't care less that I was late for work. She was a totally different person sober, desperate for more drugs, geeked out, or whatever she was. And I of course wasn't in an amorous mood. I was preoccupied with my missing car, not having my keys, being late for work, the feeling in my head, the taste in my mouth, the shower I knew I wouldn't have time to take, and the money I went through last night. For some reason, I never thought about the *good* time we had.

I was going to call the bar and let Karen, the day bartender, know I was going to be a few minutes late. I went into the bathroom first to clean myself up the best I could. I looked at the monster in the mirror. I looked the way I felt—like death. I washed my face quickly and found an empty tube of Crest. I managed to squeeze enough toothpaste onto my forefinger to give myself a finger brushing. I always carried an overnight bag in the trunk of my car containing a change of clothes and hygiene products—yes, my lifestyle did demand that I do this—but obviously I didn't have it.

I quickly hurried into the bedroom to finish dressing. I pulled up the bootstraps of my Durangos and, preoccupied with my predicament, thought about the money I had spent last night. I pulled out my wallet from the rear pocket of my jeans to double check how much money was really in there. I still remembered having fifty dollars—but it was gone. My money was gone. I forgot about calling Karen and stormed out of the bedroom to cross-examine Jules about the missing money from my wallet. She was entering the bedroom at the same time and we crashed into each other.

"Where's my money?" I said.

"What money? I don't know what you're talking about," she said, furrowing her brow and contorting her face into contempt.

"The fifty dollars I knew I had in my wallet before I fell asleep."

"How the fuck should I know? It's your fucking wallet."

"What is going on around here? You stole my money, didn't you?

You fucking stole my money."

"I didn't *steal* your money. We didn't think you'd mind. I didn't want to wake you. Bill went to get more."

"More what? Haven't you had enough?"

"Fuck off!" she yelled and retreated to the living room area.

I chased after her. "Come here." I grabbed her by the upper arm.

She squirmed trying to break my hold. "Chill out, you fucking creep," she said as she hit me in the face with her free hand.

The lustful erotic rounds of raw sex on an early morning bed turned into a hateful afternoon of belligerent animosity. I had hit a girl only once in my life for something I can't remember now. It was during high school days when I was growing up in Port Chester, New York. I slapped Patty DeLuca. She told her father and consequently the old man didn't take it too lightly. He gave me a convincing warning that he'd kill me if I ever laid my hands on his daughter again. It was a good lesson. I took it to heart. I never touched a girl again with any physical force until this hung over, car missing, keys gone, money stolen, late for work, no shower, rainy for the first time in thirty-two days, feeling like shit, not myself afternoon.

I yanked Jules's arm, dragging her feet from my left to right side. She resisted by punching me in the neck. I slapped her across the face. She tried to punch me again but I deflected her swing.

"Fucking asshole," she screamed out.

I walloped her again. This time she *smiled* and gurgled a low-toned laugh. "This how you get your kicks? You'll never see your car now. K Dog has it."

I went into a rage.

I grabbed Jules by the throat, picked up her hundred-and-twenty-pound body with my right shaking hand and nailed her against the non-painted, non-wallpapered wall. I held her there.

"You fucking bitch," I shouted into bulging white eyes.

Her feet were dangling three feet from the floor.

Normally at about this time, I would be sliding the cash drawer into the register and making my first rum 'n' Coke for Craig, the Pacific Gas & Electric man, on his way home from work. Instead, I was strangling a woman.

Jules's face turned violet-blue. Her eyes bugged out, looking searchingly into mine, not with sexual seduction as she had done only hours before, but with a pathetic silent plea for me to let her live. It was this look and realization of what I was doing that finally alerted my better sense of judgment. I let go. She dropped to the floor with a thud.

Jules gasped, gagged, and coughed.

"Hit me again, Mickey," were the first words out of her out-of-breath lungs.

I stood there panting and gasping for breath myself. I was terribly shaken and surprised at myself for almost killing her. I stepped back, looked around, and found keys on a pile of *Vogue* and *Cosmopolitan* magazines. Jules was groping for her breath on the floor among the videos, "Sheila Sucks Charlotte," and "Forbidden Sex Angels in Hell." I swung open the front door, glared at Jules and told her that I wanted my car, keys, and money returned to me at the bar. I then kicked the screen door right off its one lamed hanging hinge and took the Datsun.

I couldn't get the vision of Jules's helpless, dying eyes out of my mind as I backed out of the driveway with dangerous reverse speed. I sped down that pleasant oleander and eucalyptus street thinking worst-case scenarios about my Mustang. It was the first brand new car I had ever owned. It took long nights of saying "no" to save enough money for the down payment. I loved that car.

At the stop sign at the end of the street, I turned left and drove east towards McDee's. My mind whirled unsteadily. I couldn't get the image of Jules's masochistic smile out of my mind. She liked it. She liked me hitting her. And then the sex and cocaine and music came back to me... *tangled in a web* ...

33

3

As I opened the rear entrance door, twenty-five minutes late for work, Dottie was on her way out. She didn't care one way or the other if the night bartenders were late. We had to deal with answering to the day bartender, who in this case was Karen. Since this was only the second time I had been late in weeks, I knew Karen wouldn't be too upset; however, I had just remembered that I never called her.

"Hi Dottie, sorry I'm late," I said as I breezed past her, hurrying to reach the employee door which would connect me backstage behind the bar. I still felt I owed my boss an apology.

"Oh, Mickey…"

I stopped and turned.

"There was a girl in here last night, now I don't know if you knew it or not, but she's not supposed to be in here. Her name's Jules. Lukens, I think her last name is. She's a short blonde-haired little gal, she's—"

"I know who you're talking about. She entered the tournament… won one round, lost the second. She left after that. I'm sorry, I didn't know she wasn't supposed to be in here."

"That's okay. But *she* knows."

"If she comes in again, I'll ask her to leave."

"Good. I'm going home."

As Dottie turned to leave I asked, "What'd she do to get eighty-sixed?"

"Stole a car from the parking lot. We can't prove it was her, but the people she came in with were the ones who got caught. I just don't want her in here anymore, okay?"

"Sure, whatever you say."

Dottie turned and walked out and mumbled, "One of those things," as though she had seen everything there is to see owning and running a bar. The door closed behind her.

I stood for a moment in more of a daze than I'd stumbled in with. Will I have to force Jules into getting my Mustang back by more intimidation and strangulation? At least I knew where she lived. I looked over at Karen, who already had started her register ring-out. The stench of beer made me feel like I never left the place. I felt like vomiting.

"Hi," Karen smiled.

"Sorry," I said expectantly, "I was going to call…"

"It's okay, don't worry about it."

The bar was empty except for Craig, the Pacific Gas & Electric man; Ed, a teamster transportation captain; and Harold, a retired grumpy old redneck. I knew they were there when I drove into the parking lot; I recognized all their cars. I didn't like Harold and he didn't like me. He went too far to bust my balls. He and Ed were old enough to be my father. Both were veterans of World War II-and-don't-you-ever-forget-it-son. Craig was our other Vietnam vet resident. No flashbacks, no crazy flare-ups, just a lot of drinking.

"I told Dottie to fire you for being late," was Harold's comforting contribution to making me feel worse than I already felt.

"No, he didn't," Karen said smiling, as she pulled out the cash drawer and tore off the register's printout. She would now go into the back employees' room, count the money, deposit it in the safe, and leave. Karen was a model bartender: she knew how to mix a good cocktail, had a sweet disposition, always smiled, chatted sincerely with the customers and left them alone when they needed to be. She was a good looker, too. I always fantasized dating her, or more specifically, fucking her. But she had too many boyfriends (none of which were McDee's customers).

35

I slipped my own cash drawer into the register. I didn't bother counting to make sure I was starting with three hundred dollars. I didn't care and slammed the drawer into the register.

"Where the hell you get that piece of junk?" Harold asked, referring to the Datsun they all had seen me park while watching on the security monitor.

Ed, the polite and laid-back California native and ex-magazine writer for *Hot Rod Magazine*, *Motortrend*, and *Car & Driver* stared down into his standard on-his-way-home Southern Comfort on the rocks. "Leave the son alone," Ed said.

Harold made a comment *sotto voce*. I knew the comment was aimed at me.

"Hey, Harold, I'm in no mood for you tonight, okay?"

"Uh-oh, somebody woke up in the wrong bed today," Craig chided, not realizing how close he hit to the problem at hand. "Aren't those the same clothes you wore yesterday?"

I didn't answer.

"Where's your fancy car?" Harold asked, not letting up.

"Blew a valve. That's why I'm late… had to borrow a friend's car," I lied. I hated lying. I also hated having to explain things. Tending bar you can't get away. You could walk away for the moment, but you can't get away.

There was silence. The jukebox offered no music. The clacking of billiard balls against each other and hard cushioned felt was non-existent. The television's sound was turned off as usual. Tom Brokaw was talking into thin air.

"Son, turn this up a bit," Ed said.

I grabbed the remote control and turned up the volume:

> Today the Los Angeles Police Department hired a new chief, Philadelphia Police Commissioner Willie L. Williams. He is to succeed embattled Chief Daryl F. Gates as the department's top official; it was announced today by Los Angeles Mayor Tom Bradley in the wake of the Rodney King beating March third of last year.

The newscast now showed Mayor Bradley at a press conference announcing the news.

The men watched. I brooded.

Williams was on the screen:

> I fully understand and realize the concerns, the worries, the needs and, most importantly, the love and affection that each and every one of you has for this city and this outstanding Police Department.

The men all laughed after Williams said, "...love and affection..."

All I could think about was my own embattlement not more than an hour ago and how I wanted – no, needed – a blast of high-octane cocaine. It'd be just a matter of time before Bones or one of the other dealers arrived. Bones was probably having one of his girls grill him a steak. Yeah, nice guy that Bones, but don't you ever dare cross him.

No one of any importance showed their face before seven o'clock except for the present crew, a couple of stragglers, and a few guys on their way home who'd stop in first before kissing the wife and then sinking into their favorite lounging chair for a night of remote control, beer, and passing out. Losers, all of them.

I picked up the phone to give Jules a call and realized I didn't know her number. It was at this time that I heard Harold whisper to Craig something about "...damn New Yorkers...."

I swung around, "Look, Harold, I don't need to take this crap from you tonight, so back off."

The stillness in the air clung onto every word Brokaw was reporting about the Rodney King affair on which Harold and the others had now absent-mindedly transfixed their eyes.

I knew immediately I was wrong shouting at Harold. I certainly had handled worse harassment more diplomatically from rude inconsiderate customers. No one said a word for a long while until rational Ed cleared his throat, "You know, this guy Williams looks like a pretty decent guy."

"Should've stayed in Philadelphia," Craig softly uttered.

Everyone shifted on their barstools and sipped on their drinks, waiting for relief in a change of subject or for something to happen that allows people in embarrassing moments to act natural again.

I reached for a bar towel, walked away from the men, and cleaned an area of the bar which didn't need cleaning.

It finally was me who provided the aforementioned relief. "Listen, Harold, I'm sorry I yelled at you." The men shifted on their barstools again. Ed smiled to himself and so did Craig.

"Aww, that's okay," Harold said, surprised by my apology. I was surprised by his humbleness.

"Let me buy you a beer," I said and placed a shot glass upside down in front of Harold, indicating the coming of a free drink. "I've been having a bad day," I said to the men in general.

Harold feigned a smile and looked down into his beer glass. I felt sorry for him.

I poured each of us a shot I knew we all drank: Irish Mist.

We clinked our glasses in ceremonious forgiveness.

I shook hands with Harold and someone cut a joke, I think it was Craig, that Harold was an asshole anyway. We all had a good laugh.

Minutes later, we all heard the distinct rumbling of a Harley-Davidson motorcycle. Gary dismounted from his bike and wandered in. Even though he and Craig knew of their common bond of being Vietnam veterans, they never talked about it. Gary seemed shell-shocked and Craig didn't want to go down that jungle patch with him. They said their "helloes" and it never went further than that. Maybe Craig understood what Gary had gone through and left it alone. After all, spending sixteen months as a prisoner of war—four of which were spent in solitary confinement—will make anyone crazy. While in solitary, Gary talked to himself to keep from going nuts. Even now, once in a while when he was alone, sitting somewhere off to the side, flashbacks and the world heavy on his large-framed shoulders, stroking his black and gray beard, waiting patiently for his turn during a game of eight ball, you'd find him mumbling to himself. And when he talked to you and you looked into his eyes it looked like someone else was driving. Gary never touched drugs. Jack Daniel was his sponsor.

Gary reached for his Jack 'n' Coke and threw down a five at the same time. He practiced pool shots by himself. The drunker he got, the better he'd shoot. It was frightening.

Every time the phone rang I answered with anticipation of it being Jules telling me she was on her way to exchange cars and to pay me back. She never called, and as the time passed I felt a deeper sinking feeling in my gut that I would never see my Mustang again. Who really had my car? Bill or K Dog?

Of course, I couldn't tell anyone what really happened. It would have been too embarrassing, especially the way rumors fly in the neighborhood bar business. I knew telling anyone the truth would have made me look like an idiot. *Hey, did you hear about Mickey getting his money stolen and his car ripped off while he was sleeping with Jules?* Peter would love it.

Saloon rumors. Nothing to do but yak, yak, yak when you're sitting at the bar tossing down a few or six. Nothing to do but joke and laugh about other people and their problems and misfortunes.

"Jules? You mean the one in the Laundromat?" Gary answered after I asked him what he knew of her.

"What are you talking about?"

"I don't know, she did some guy in a dryer she met at one of those twenty-four hour Laundromats."

"What the fuck are you talking about—in the dryer?"

"She sat in the dryer, he stood there, and she gave him a blow job," Gary said and smiled crazy-like. "I don't think it was spinning, though."

"In the dryer," I stated for the record.

"She's small enough."

"I guess."

"Can I have another drink, please?"

❁   ❁   ❁

"So, I hear you're going out with Jules," Jamie proclaimed as she plopped down on the barstool and slung her handbag onto the empty stool next to her.

I just looked at her.

"What?" Jamie finally asked.

"Now I'm 'going out' with her?"

"Whatever. My usual, please."

I mixed Jamie an Absolut and cranberry juice while cursing to myself. She lit a Marlboro Light and took a hard first drag, "You know, she's bad news."

"Worse than you?"

Jamie cracked a smile. Smoke came out from between her fat lips. "Yeah, worse than me. Ashley, get down!"

Ashley, Jamie's seven-year-old daughter, was climbing a nearby barstool.

"Go sit over there, honey," Jamie said.

I made a Shirley Temple for Ashley. "Here, sweetheart." I gave it to her. She sat down in one of the booths. I gave Jamie a look.

"We're not staying, I just came in for *one* drink," Jamie explained. She sipped at it. "Well?"

"Well what?"

"Since I know you did her, is she better than me?"

"I'm not going to answer that." Jamie laughed to herself again. "How would you know if I did her?"

"C'mon, Mickey," she snickered. Her and Peter: the snickerers.

She took another sip of her cocktail and drag off her cigarette. She tossed her long bleached-blonde hair back over her right shoulder, a habit she'd done a million times. "But I still love you."

"I'm a little strung out right now, do you have anything?"

"I thought you quit."

"I did, but that was last week, remember?"

"See what she's doing to you?"

"Nothing you didn't do to me."

"Nothing you didn't want done to you."

"Do me now."

Jamie turned around and looked at Ashley, who was preoccupied dipping her straw and playing with the handful of cherries I gave her in the ginger ale and grenadine. Jamie reached into her handbag and covertly handed me an amber vial. I immediately went into the back room, closed the door, and snorted two giant hits.

There's a woman in every bar in every town across America like Jamie. They're single mothers, bleached-blonde, alcoholics, unemployed, hating themselves and their world. They drown themselves in booze, drugs, and sex. They'd soon fuck you, rob you of your money, and seduce you into their world until they've gotten everything they can from you. Jamie wasn't a bad looker, just the pain of life had scarred her used body.

Jamie was the first girl I fucked after getting the job at McDee's. It was my first night there. Everyone, including Charlene, had gone. Over a couple of powerful Absoluts Jamie came on to me, and before the eastern light made its vital force of the day we did what all bartenders do after hours alone with a girl like Jamie, we screwed on the pool table.

While Jamie was on her third drink and Ashley on her fifth, more cast members had started strolling in. It was eight-thirty. But the place wouldn't get busy until after nine o'clock.

❀   ❀   ❀

I was trapped behind the bar. *Hey, Dottie, by the way, I had to leave the bar for an hour or so to go look for my car. I just told everyone to help themselves with their drinks. Sort of like a party. You don't mind, do ya? And, oh, after they arrest me for killing Jules, can you bail me out of jail, por favor?"* It was a good thing Peter wasn't in that night. I would have had to answer a lot of questions.

Charlene: "How was your *date*? You look like shit."

❀   ❀   ❀

It wasn't until two-thirty that night—or morning, however you want to look at it—when I was alone, ready to walk out the door to drive over to Jules's house, when out of the corner of my eye up on the security monitor I saw the headlights of a Mustang turn into the parking lot and drive up to the rear door. The top was down, of course. Jules beeped the horn, stood on the seat, and waved into the camera's lens sending scattered pixel signals into the monitor. She then jumped over the driver's side door while leaving the lights on and the car idling. That's when I walked out. I recognized the all-too-familiar music blasting from the car's speakers. Besides the CD she had an audiocassette, too.

Jules rushed over to me and gave me a smile and a hug as though nothing had happened. "Hi, honey bunny," she said to me.

I pushed her out of the way and walked around the car inspecting it for dents and damages. I found none.

"I got a surprise for you," Jules said proudly.

"Now I'm your honey bunny?"

"Yeah, why? Don't you wanna be?"

"Where was my car all night?"

"In my driveway. You just missed Bill. If you had waited three more minutes instead of trying to kill me, you would have—"

"I don't believe you," I interrupted.

"Believe what you want. I'm here, aren't I? With your car? Why, where you gonna go? You're working. I figured I'd just bring it to you when you got out of work. Something wrong with that?"

I sat behind the steering wheel, ejected the tape and threw the cassette over my shoulder into the back seat. I looked at the gas indicator needle: E. I then looked at the odometer. Quite frankly, I didn't know what the mileage was or how much gas I'd had before I went over to Jules's house, but I said anyway, "Somebody's been driving around."

"Well, you knew that," Jules answered matter-of-factly and then climbed over the wheel and straddled herself right on top of me with her thin frame, perfumed and seductive. She was dressed with only a pink camisole and faded cut-off Sasson jeans. Her tits dangled in my face. That's all she had on, no shoes, no bra, no jewelry. She laughed and started kissing my right ear lobe. It turned me on. She stuck her tongue down my throat. I didn't resist. My anger subsided and I kissed back, hard.

"You really hurt me today. All I was trying to do was get you something so you'd feel better when you woke up. I didn't know you had to work tonight," she said and kissed me again. My cock stiffened. "Lock up and let's go to my place," she said while getting off me and jumping into the passenger seat. She opened up the glove compartment and pulled out her pipe. It was obvious she was getting impatient to have another hit, even though she had probably taken her most recent hit only eight minutes ago, a minute before she left her house.

"Wait. Not here, okay? You're a piece of work, you know that?" I shut off the car's lights and the engine. "We'll go inside, everybody's gone."

4

Depression set in as soon as I turned my key in the tumbler, unlocking the door of my one bedroom apartment. Jules and I had stayed at the bar drinking, smoking, and screwing, and scampered out of there before the clean-up guy arrived at six a.m. Jules drove her "unregistered" Datsun home and I had my Mustang back. The sparrows and finches were chirping to the beginning of another sunny day in Sherman Oaks, where my apartment was located. I hadn't slept much the last forty-eight hours, but I felt wide-awake—too wide-awake. I was wired and didn't know what to do with myself.

The answering machine's flashing red LED indicated five new messages.

My dad had called asking why he and my mom hadn't heard from me in a while; there was a hang-up; Tropical Cruises left a computer out-going-message which went on and on about how *YOU, Mister Michael Collins*, may have won a cruise if *YOU, Mister Michael Collins*, attend the seminar next week at the Marriott Hotel in Woodland Hills, *blah, blah, blah*; another hang-up; and a message from the landlord reminding *YOU, Mister Michael Collins,* your rent is overdue.

I stared at the stack of overdue bills accumulating next to the answering machine. I made a good living working four shifts and bringing home between six hundred and seven hundred dollars per week; but with car payments, insurance, groceries, gas and electric, telephone, dating women, drinking, buying drugs, hiring an occasional prostitute, well, it just wasn't enough.

I opened the refrigerator door and realized I hadn't eaten in two days. I wasn't hungry then, either. I flopped down on the bed and stared at the ceiling. Partying, staying up late, leading a life of debauchery, and not getting the requisite Rapid Eye Movement can knock a person out. I was more tired than I'd thought. I fell asleep in the clothes I had been wearing for two days.

When I awoke I was still in the same position—boots and all. I'd slept only a couple of hours but felt refreshed and wide awake. That's the way it is with cocaine. You might be able to fall asleep, but after you wake up the drug is still in your system and you're ready to go, go, go. It's the following day that knocks you out.

My apartment at the Regal Courts, in Sherman Oaks, was between a three to four mile distance from McDee's. Sherman Oaks is an excellent location on "that" side of the hill. Los Angeles proper, Hollywood, Beverly Hills, and Santa Monica being the "other" side of the hill. The *hill* is actually part of a mountain range that divides the San Fernando Valley from Los Angles and is considered part of the Santa Monica Mountains, which extend westward, nowhere near Santa Monica, but close enough—Westwood, Brentwood, and Malibu. This low mountain range is only a half mile from the Regal Courts, and on a clear smogless day you can actually see this green lush hill, houses supported on stilts, peppered in between the steep cliffs, canyons, monkey palms, hibiscus shrubs, and eucalyptus trees.

The Regal Courts has its own underground parking garage, hot tub, pool, and workout room—all the amenities of a Southern California apartment complex.

Since I had to work that night, I wanted to take it slow and relax for the day. I rode the elevator downstairs to the pool, to lie in the sun, hoping I could fall back to sleep again. I listened to the cars and trucks and buses and motorcycles speed up and down Van Nuys Boulevard.

I closed my eyes, but I couldn't sleep because my mind was racing. Where did Jules and girls like her come from? what were their childhoods like? did they love their fathers? did their fathers love them back? did their fathers love them back too much? Recent news in the *Times*... gang members from South Central Los Angeles were arrested for killing a three-year-old girl... what's the average life expectancy living in South Central? Dodgers lost to the Houston Astros... Bill Clinton is running for president... a murderer named Robert Alton Harris is going to die in the gas chamber next week if he doesn't receive a clemency... will the four Los Angeles Police Department officers who "allegedly" beat Rodney King be acquitted?

❀   ❀   ❀

On Sunday, I took Jules out for something like a date. Again, it was another warm, clear and sunny day. By anyone's standards it was a perfect day. This is what California is all about, driving through the canyons and along the Pacific Coast Highway with the top down, having a good time. To me, nothing equals this except what goes along with it at the end of the day: a cool shower, a few Tanqueray 'n' tonics at sunset, a prime rib dinner, a bottle of red wine, and making love.

We took the Los Virgenes Malibu Exit off the Ventura Freeway. Instead of continuing straight towards the coast which was less than two miles away, I made a right onto Mulholland Drive and followed the route I rode when I had my own Harley, before I spilled it speeding down Laurel Canyon Boulevard misnegotiating a turn in front of where Jim Morrison once lived and where it's still written on the gray cement wall in black paint: Mr. Mojo Man. We drove past the Rock Store (actually a small grocery store) where on any Sunday afternoon one hundred motorcycles would be parked and lined up, their owners swapping road stories.

Jules had never been on this road before nor had she been to the beach in the time she had been living in Los Angeles. No, mostly she'd been in other places, dark places, hiding places. Jail.

We ended up at the Malibu Inn and ordered a couple of burgers and beers for lunch. Jules gulped the burger down before I got halfway through with mine.

We played pool.

"No guy ever beat me three games in a row," she said, sidling up to me, impressed with my gamesmanship.

"What's my reward?"

"What do you want it to be?"

I thought about Laundromats.

She walked away, her ass inside her vermilion day-glow Bonjour short-shorts purposefully moving from side to side. She was wearing a matching short-short tank top, her shoulders bare and belly button vulnerable. She chalked her cue as seductively as anyone could possibly chalk a cue. "I don't do that," she said teasingly, reading my mind once again.

"Let's get out of here," I said as I gingerly placed my cue down on the table.

She placed her cue down next to mine.

I wrapped my arms around her skinny lower back and darted my tongue against hers. Wet kisses.

We walked across Pacific Coast Highway to the beach and laid out on a blanket I also kept in the trunk of my Mustang. We sat and stared out at the surfers.

"This is nice," she said, taking it all in. Her body was embarrassingly white due to living at night. I managed a tan from March till December.

The sun pounded our bodies with heat and radiation. I felt content.

"You know, you never told me where you're from," I said into her Donna Karan sunglasses.

"Kansas City," she said into my Ray Bans.

"What brought you to La-La-Land?"

"I moved here with a boyfriend. He wanted to be a musician. Well, he was, is, a musician."

"What happened?"

"Caught him screwing some actress or model or whatever she was."

"How'd you meet Stephanie?"

"Met her at a party. We hit it off. She'd just broken up with her boyfriend, too, and was looking for another place to live. She said her brother, Bill, might let us move in with him. He got hurt on his job. He's an auto mechanic… started collecting disability and needed someone to share the expenses."

"He seems like a nice guy."

"Bill's a jerk."

"He let you move in…"

"What about you? Didn't you tell me you're from New *Yawk?* Writer or something?"

"Yeah, screenwriter… came out here to work in the 'biz'. Things haven't been working out as planned."

"That business sucks. I know a few people… low-lifes if you ask me."

"What do they do?"

"Pornos."

I gave out a short laugh.

"Money's supposed to be pretty good. Thought maybe I'd try it someday. You think I'd make a good porn star?" Jules said.

"Why don't you do something useful? There're books out there supposed to help you 'find' yourself."

"The only book I ever read was *Alice in Wonderland*. I have a friend, Louie, who even calls me that. He says I remind him of Alice in Wonderland… that I always need to learn my lesson. Fuck it. I'm just going to grow old and die doing what I'm doing."

But then, thought Alice, *shall I never get any older than I am now? That'll be a comfort, one way—never to be an old woman—but then—always have lessons to learn. Oh, I shouldn't like that.*

"You can write my story, but nobody would believe it," Jules said.

"Is it stranger than fiction?"

Jules didn't answer. She left it hanging. She didn't want to tell me the story of her life at that moment. Of course her silence made me all the more curious. Then she said, "Yeah, that's a good one, stranger than fiction."

I almost wish I hadn't gone down that rabbit hole—and yet—and yet—it's rather curious, you know, this sort of life. I do wonder what can have happened to me. When I used to read fairy tales, I fancied that kind of thing never happened, and now here I am in the middle of one. There ought to be a book written about me, that there ought.

After that we didn't talk for a long while.

Early that evening we engaged in an argument at her house about me not wanting to buy cocaine. I walked out, went home, finished off a bottle of gin and fell asleep. The cool shower, prime rib dinner, bottle of wine, and lovemaking were non-existent even in my dreams.

❁ ❁ ❁

On Tuesday, Robert Alton Harris was put to death by a mist of cyanide vapors.

I paid the rent.

That same night I couldn't stop thinking about Jules. I replayed our drug-induced sexual aerobics, the good time we had at the beach on Sunday, and forgot about the fight we had.

Bones gave me a deal of three vials for a hundred dollars as a surprise to cook up with Jules. Maybe Stephanie would be there and the three of us could get *tangled in a web*.

I was driving west towards Jules's house and was approaching the intersection of Victory and Sepulveda Boulevards when I saw Jules in the Datsun making a left turn on the opposite side of Victory onto Sepulveda. She didn't see me because she was looking north in the direction she was driving.

I swerved into the right lane, made the turn, and followed her. I kept a few car lengths behind so she couldn't see me. She continued north. It wasn't until she approached Roscoe Boulevard, in Panorama City, that I supposed a drug purchase. She made a left onto a side street. By the time I made the left she had already curbed the Datsun. I pulled over to the right and watched her cross the street, not bothering to pull her silver spandex dress down. She scooted into a small white stucco red-tiled roof house. Boxwood hedges, honeysuckle bushes, and jacaranda trees lined the street. I lit a Marlboro.

I heard a loud *pop* from the house from which Jules was now quickly running. She reached the street when a Mexican hombre from inside the house came out after her. Jules turned and a small bright flare exploded from her hand—a gun. She shot the Mexican and didn't bother sticking around to watch him fall down on the front lawn. She jumped into her car and sped down the street, finally turning the headlights on after she went through the stop sign and made a left.

I couldn't believe what I had just witnessed. I sat there in shock before realizing I should get the hell out of there. I quickly made a U-turn. By the time I reached the beginning of the street she had already made a right from the next street over and pulled into the stream of traffic, almost causing an accident. She sped ahead, passing cars on her right and left. I had to stop for a red signal. I thought about the consequences now of being connected with Jules. Would I somehow be implicated in this crime as an "accessory" if I didn't come forward to the police and tell them what I saw? Have I now become a "star" player in her drama—her life? Was this supposed to be some sort of true-life script now playing out? A *soon to be major motion picture*?

I drove past her house—but no Datsun. I parked down the street out of sight and waited for her return. I still couldn't believe what I had seen. Was the Mexican dead, or hopefully, just wounded? What was his and Jules's connection, their backstory? Was the shooting over drugs? An hour went by. Still no Datsun.

When I turned the key to enter my apartment I didn't hear or feel the familiar sound of the tumbler unlocking. I cautiously opened the door and saw Jules sitting on the sofa with one of my towels wrapped around her body, watching the news, and smoking a cigarette. Her hair was wet. "Hi," she said, happy to see me.

"Hi," I answered her, hiding mixed emotions running rampant inside me. "How'd *you* get in?" I asked obviously surprised.

"Door was unlocked."

I examined the door and lock to see if somehow she broke in. I did not believe I'd left my apartment without locking the door.

"How did you know where I lived?"

"It's on your driver's license, dummy. I looked at it the time I 'stole' your money. Remember?"

"Yeah, I remember. I also remember you haven't paid me back."

"Haven't I given you enough?"

"So that's the way it is. How'd you get past the doorman?"

"Who, Freddie? Oh, we're old friends now." She laughed. "Where've you been?"

"Out," I said as I gave the apartment a once over. Everything looked in order. If she'd wanted to rip me off she would have done so by then. I kept cash in my apartment, and I also thought about the checkbook in the drawer of my desk. I'd look later to see if any cash or checks were missing. Her spandex dress was on the floor in the bathroom.

I attempted to act natural and not let on what I knew about the shooting. She was calm as though nothing had happened—as though she hadn't just shot a man.

"You look nervous," she said.

"I obviously didn't expect to see you here. Why?"

"I just wanted to surprise you."

That you did.

I walked into the kitchen. A box of baking soda I kept in the refrigerator was on the counter next to the gas range. A spoon and the workings of freebasing paraphernalia were also on the counter top.

"Well, I hope you're comfortable," I said, reentering the living room area.

She stood up, the towel wrapped around her body falling to the floor. She stood there naked and put a chunk of rock in her pipe. She handed it to me. "Nice place you got here."

I desperately wanted to take a hit but there was something inside of me telling me no. I took the hit anyway and handed the pipe back to her. We fucked on the sofa, then on the floor. After a while she said she "had to go and do something."

I said, "Okay."

She got dressed, handed me some rocks and was out the door. I checked the drawer where I kept my cash and checkbook. I didn't know how much cash I should have had but there were six twenties. No checks were missing.

I sat down on the sofa, took out the coke vials I had in my pocket, played with them in the palm of my hand, lit a cigarette, and decided not to sees Jules ever again.

5

Wednesday, an earthquake with the magnitude of 6.1 rolled through Southern California. High-rise office buildings swayed for thirty seconds in downtown Los Angeles and Century City. Strong shock waves were felt from Las Vegas to San Diego.

That night, while working, I got a frantic phone call from Jules. The call had nothing to do with the quake earlier in the day, but I detected a shaking in her voice. "I need you," she immediately said after I answered the phone.

"Yeah, I've been thinking about you, too," I said to her. I didn't tell her I was thinking about the shooting rather than amorous thoughts. Earlier in the day, I turned the pages in the Valley section of the *Los Angeles Times* and the entire *Daily News* to see if I could find any reports of shootings. There weren't any. If she had killed whomever it was she had shot, there would have been something in the paper. I watched the local news on television at the bar. Nothing was mentioned of anyone getting killed on their front lawn in Panorama City.

"I'm scared," she admitted.

Jules couldn't be scared of anything, but she didn't sound right. "What's the matter?" I asked, genuinely concerned.

"Somebody called today and said they were going to kill me."

I wasn't surprised, but I acted like I was. "Do you have any idea who—"

53

"Can you meet me after work?" Jules interrupted.

"Where?" I asked, assuming she was at home.

"At the Wayfarer."

The Wayfarer is a motel on Sepulveda Boulevard not far from where Jules lived. It was a local hangout for prostitutes, dealers, users, the general low-life, and Asian businessmen who either knew or didn't know the Wayfarer's reputation. Before I could answer she gave me the room number.

"I'm in room two-thirty-seven."

"What do you want me to do?"

"Just be here for me."

"I won't be able to get there till about two-thirty or three."

"Hurry, okay?"

I didn't know what, or who, I would find at the Wayfarer. The shooting incident was the obvious threat of retaliation. However, Jules had a lot of enemies. She owed people money, drugs, favors; maybe there were other shootings. Most girls didn't like her. They were threatened by her forwardness, good looks, savvyness, and her ability to steal away their boyfriends. The men who hated her were the ones she had either burned in drug deals, or the ones to whom she wouldn't succumb and they resented her, or those who loved her but somehow got misled. She put men down, ran circles around them, and carried them along on a leash, using them and then tossing them away like Raggedy Andys when she was done. She poked holes in them like they were living voodoo dolls and then she would lay them aside, their hearts punctured, bleeding. It was Bill who brought this pattern to my attention one night that *all* the men Jules had dated were violent. "Maybe they weren't violent before they met her," I said to him. He laughed and said that maybe I was right. We both knew it was easy to get angry with Jules, but it was *her* behavior that caused men to flare up. She had been beaten, kicked, raped, and thrown from cars. She was able to bring out the worst in any man— the worst in me. I tried to kill her. I wasn't like that. Not at all. She did something to me to cause me to choke her that late afternoon. She had a power to extract the dark side of a man and then relish in his demise like a black widow spider that kills her unsuspecting victim after she has her way with him. *Tangled in a web.* Men preceding me ended up with restraining orders to stay away from her. There were car crashes, near deaths, busts by the police, jail, and the rumor that a cop from Chicago had fallen in love with Jules and had an affair with her while he was still married and that he was looking for Jules and determined to find her because she stole money from him. How could I possibly love someone like her? Maybe it was infatuation. Maybe I was making a big mistake. But it hurt so good, I didn't understand.

❀   ❀   ❀

When I approached two-thirty-seven I heard loud music, Black Sabbath, and people laughing. I boldly knocked on the door.
"Who is it?" a muffled voice asked. It was Jules.
"Mickey."
Jules opened the door and I walked into a smoke-filled room. There were two guys and one other girl besides Jules. Jules was happy as a bee, buzzing just the same.
"I thought you were in trouble," I said.
"I am," she said smiling and then spinned. Again with the spinning.
"Don't spin, okay? Who are these people?" I asked softly.
"Friends I just met."
"Get them out."
"Okay," she answered without any fanfare of an argument.
She turned to her new acquaintances and told them to leave. They left peacefully. I lowered the volume on the same battle-ridden boom box she had kept in her bedroom.
"So, why did you call me? Doesn't look like you're in any kind of trouble."
"I got protection," Jules said proudly. She turned the volume up on her boom box after I had just turned it down and then she paced in front of the full-length mirror fastened to the outside of the bathroom

door. She was wearing taillight-red hot pants and a gumball-blue tube top. She proceeded to play with her hair and gazed lovingly at herself. She cupped the cheeks of her own ass with both hands, stood on her naked toes and spinned.

"*Protection*? From who?" I lowered the music again.

"From the guy who's paying for this room." She inspected her face in the mirror as though she had never seen her own image before.

I tried not to sound bothered. "So why do you need me?"

"I just thought you might want to *be* with *me*."

"Look, next time—if there is a next time—don't tell me you're in trouble just to get me—"

"What do you mean 'if there is a next time'?" she said, staring into the reflection of her own eyes, "Did you bring me anything?"

I tried to remember which pocket my stash was in. "No."

Jules looked at me and said, "Hmmp." She then returned her attention to herself in the mirror as if something physically had changed in the interim of the last two seconds.

I sat and watched her strut in front of the mirror again. There was an evil I saw in her that attracted me and made me keep coming back—even though I knew she was bad for me. She held the markings of a mystery I wanted to solve, and now I was a player, a character in this twisted movie.

"Who *is* this protection?" I pressed.

"Some guy I know."

"You fucking him?"

"Nooo." She turned from the mirror and stared into my eyes. "Even if I was, would it make a difference? It's not like we're married to each other or anything."

Thank God, I said to myself.

She entered the bathroom to her self-made vanity in front of the bathroom sink's mirror and applied more mascara to her eyelashes.

"So, where is he?" I asked her.

"Who?"

Jesus. "This *protection*."

"At my house."

"Excuse me, but what are you doing here if your *protection's* at your house? Do you think the Wayfarer is a good place to hide out? I mean if someone is looking for you, don't you think they'd look here?"

"I never come here. Stephanie does. I don't. And stop saying 'protection' like you're mocking me. I told you someone called me to say they were going to kill me."

I'd been wanting to ask her about the shooting. Now was the time, but I reconsidered. I figured hidden knowledge is power. I knew something about her she didn't think I knew. Prison, stealing cars, Laundromats, and now the shooting. God, what was I getting in to?

"We're not staying here, anyway," Jules informed me as she strutted out of the bathroom and shut off and unplugged her boom box.

"Where we going?"

"To go visit my *protection*."

"Brilliant."

❀ ❀ ❀

Jules drove with me since she didn't have transportation. Her boom box and a small Gucci handbag sat on her lap. It took us three minutes to get to her house. Parked in the driveway behind the Datsun this time was a brand new white 1992 Cadillac Seville. Nevada plates. Jules knocked three times, paused, and then knocked once—a secret code. As we both waited for the locked door to open, I looked down at the screen door lying lamely half off the porch, half on the grass—just where it lay after I had kicked it off its one hinge.

Bill opened the door.

We entered and immediately heard the high sweet shrill of a mezzo-soprano. Opera music. Jules closed the door and we both stood transfixed at the scene before us. A large heavyset man wearing a barbecue apron tied snugly around himself was picking up trash from the floor and putting it inside a large black plastic garbage bag. The barbecue apron showed a picture of a cow. Above the cow were the words, "I'm in the pits." Underneath the apron a leather holster sling with what looked liked a 9mm automatic was also strapped tightly to the man. He was cleaning up the place. Bill was helping. The music was coming from a sparkling new Panasonic CD player. Its newly opened box sat on the floor in the center of the room now filled with videocassettes, "Tammy's Tricks," et cetera.

"This is interesting," Jules said. She looked at me and laughed.

"This is your—"

"Shush," she warned me.

The man stopped what he was doing and glared at Jules and me. "Quiet! This is the best part." He then went over to the CD player and raised the volume gently. We all stood there not moving for about five seconds and listened to the high-pitched woman's voice electronically emanating from the speakers. Jules made a move.

"Don't move," the man said. "*Listen.*"

We stood there motionless for almost two minutes and listened to what I imagined a humming bird would sound like if it could sing. It was the most beautiful music I had ever heard. The man himself lipped the Italian-sounding words, his expression contorted into agonizing pain and sorrow. He lifted his hands every now and then as if silently conducting to himself.

We were listening to Abbé Prévost's *Manon Lescaut,* set to music by Giacomo Puccini, Louie Vicente told us after he had lowered the music and gave us all permission to once again move.

"O mia dimora umile, tu mi ritorni innanzi gaia, isolata, bianca come un sogno gentile di pace e d'amor!" Louie-the-poet-the-opera-fanatic-the-*protection* said to Jules.

"Oh, yeah?" she answered back.

"Beautiful," I said, really meaning it.

Louie ignored me. He repeated the words again to Jules, this time in English: "O, my humble little dwelling, you return before me… happy, secluded, innocent like a gentle dream of peace and love."

I laughed.

"What's so funny?" Louie glared at me.

"Jules. ...gentle dream of peace and love."

Jules and Bill both laughed this time.

"Who are *you*?" he asked me.

"Nobody. I'm nobody."

"Louie, this is Mickey. I told you about Mickey. He's okay," Jules finally making introductions.

Louie came over to me and stood inches from my nose, studying my eyes. I looked into the blackness of his. I thought he was going to kill me right then and there.   "You thought the music was 'beautiful'?" he asked me.

"I've never heard such sweetness before in my life."

A smile came to Louie. I had a friend for life.

"This place is a pigsty," Louie said as he turned to thrash the trash. "Let's go, everybody pitch in."

"I've got other things to do," Jules said.

"Hey! You do what I say. Fuckin' place. How the fuck can you live in this garbage? What the fuck's da matter with youz?"

"Chill out," she said defiantly and stomped into her bedroom.

I looked at Bill who now was standing with a broom in his hand. He shrugged his shoulders. I went into the kitchen, passing Louie who eagerly returned to his chore. "Looks like you got things pretty much in control here," I said to Louie as I entered the kitchen. "Wow." The kitchen was immaculate, but I detected a burning chocolate aroma. "Hey, something's burning in here," I called out.

Louie rushed into the kitchen, opened the stove, pulled out a tin sheet of brownies and placed them on top of the range. He touched a few gently with the open palm of his right hand to determine their composition. "They're still good."

I didn't say anything.

He studied the brownies, then, "Whad that crazy broad tell ya 'bout me?"

"Nothing."

"She's crazy ya know."

"Yeah, I know."

I studied Louie. He was about fifty-five years old, dark

complexion, long slicked black hair combed back, gray at the temples. His face was round and fat just like the rest of him. His dark eyes, I'm sure, had seen many wars. His proclivity towards opera and cleanliness was in direct contrast to his arsenal.

"I'm in L.A. on business, came to check on Alice in Wonderland," Louie volunteered while poking a brownie with a fat forefinger.

"Hey, this is none of my business. Jules just told me she got a threatening phone call," I offered.

"You the bartender?"

"I'm the bartender."

"Fuckin' bitch is a flake. She's always getting herself into trouble. Ain't got time for *this* crap."

I just stood there. *Protection? Italian? Opera? Cadillac? Nevada plates? 9mm?*

"Are they laced?" I was referring to the brownies.

"No Mary Jane. I don't do drugs." He gave me one.

"Saved them just in time from burning," I complimented with a small mouthful.

"Damn straight," Louie said proudly, helping himself to the largest brownie. "I make the best fuckin' brownies. Mmmm, good." Brownie was falling out of his mouth. He looked at me, still with a discerning eye. "You know what opera is, kid?"

"Haven't the faintest…"

"It's life. It's love gone wrong. It's tragedy."

"What a drag."

"What a drag," Louie repeated and chuckled, liking a joke I didn't intend, "but you don't have a clue, do ya – what's your name again?"

"Mickey."

"You Italian, Mickey?"

"Irish."

"That's okay, too." He munched on his brownie. "How'd you get mixed up with Alice?"

"Just lucky, I guess."

Louie chuckled again and opened the refrigerator door to a fully stocked supply of food.

"Where all this food come from?" I asked surprised.

"Ya think I'm gonna hang out here and not have supplies? Provisions?" Louie reached for the milk and poured himself a glass—a sparkling clean glass.

"What *do* ya know?" Louie asked me, after taking a large gulp of milk.

"About what?"

"Jules. How long ya know her?"

"Just met her... been a week."

"A week!? That all? Shit. Ya know nothin'."

How about being an eyewitness to attempted murder? Does that count?

"What the fuck is she doin' in her room, drugs?"

I shrugged. "Who knows."

"You do drugs?"

I could not lie to Louie. "Sometimes."

"No good for ya. I won't allow drugs in this house while I'm here," Louie said, not making a move to go barging into Jules's room and stop her from whatever drugs she was doing. "You think she's in there now smoking that crack shit?"

"I have no idea what she's doing in her room."

"I'm telling ya, she better get her fuckin' act together. I'm not surprised somebody wants to kill her. And where's that Stephanie broad? Sex and drugs, sex and drugs, that's all that goes on around here. I don't have to tell ya."

Right, Louie, I'm part of the problem.

"Don't let her drag that cock o' yours into her mouth too many times... could get addictive, ya know? Take fuckin' control of her or she'll take control of *you*."

I thought about that. "What are you going to do?"

" 'Bout what?"

"Jules."

"Nothin'. She and I got things to talk about."

I didn't know what to do. I was silent. This was Louie's place now.

"Go check on her," Louie said. "I'll take care of things out here."
"Sure, whatever you say."
Jules's door was closed. I knocked gently. She opened it. I entered her room and we did the usual. Louie respected the closed door.

I left eight hours later. Louie was sitting in Bill's recliner, asleep. Bill was asleep somewhere else in the house, probably his room. I went home.

❀   ❀   ❀

Saturday night I went over to Jules's house after work. It was about three a.m. K Dog was there. He and Bill and Jules and Louie were sitting at the kitchen table talking. Jules asked me to wait for her in the living room. They were having a "meeting." I didn't ask about what. I watched T.J. Hooker this time chasing after armed robbers. I heard bits of conversation from the kitchen. They were talking about cars and connections and drop-off points and meeting places and money.

❀   ❀   ❀

The shouting match began Sunday morning. Jules accused Louie of stealing her gun.

"What the fuck would I want with a twenty-two caliber pistol?" Louie said as he drew his 9-millimeter automatic. He also pointed to the .357 magnum and two AK-47 assault rifles that were in full evidence.

"Where is it? I had it hidden under a pile of clothes in my room next to my bed. You go sniffing my underwear, Louie?"

"I don't sniff no underwear."

"I don't wear any."

"What are ya doin' with a gun anyway? I thought I told you a long time ago you and guns don't mix."

"Where is it?" Jules asked again, pretending not to hear what Louie was saying.

"I don't know where your fucking gun is."

"Well, somebody took it." Jules looked at Bill.

"I didn't take it," Bill said in a high-strained voice.

Jules looked at me. "I'm not fucking crazy. Somebody took my gun," she said still looking at me.

"What are you looking at me for?" I said.

Jules turned back to Louie, "Where the fuck is it?"

"I—DON'T—KNOW."

She glared at Louie.

"We're done here," Louie said to her and turned away.

Louie gathered his belongings, including the Panasonic CD player he had been listening to opera on, collected his arsenal, and mumbled that it was "Par for the course with a broad like her to be mixed up in things." Then he said to her, "I expect you to follow through on your end of the job—no fuck-ups this time," and walked out.

Jules wasn't in a good mood. We had an argument about everything.

"What did he mean about 'your end of the job'?" I asked Jules.

She told me it was none of my business and settled into a foul mood. There was no talking to her. We were without drugs, money, and booze. I left too. She'd find a gun somewhere else. Jules was resourceful like that.

6

Wednesday, April 29th. I had just kicked off my workweek by making a round of drinks for Craig, Ed, and Harold. It was one minute past six o'clock and KTLA—the station that had introduced the world to the famous Rodney King beating tape—was reporting live from the "Chopper News Team" helicopter about what would historically be known as the beginning of "The Los Angeles Riots." The TV above the bar transfixed us all. A black youth wearing a Malcolm X T-shirt had heaved a steel light pole through the window of Tom's Liquor store on the corner of Florence Avenue and Seventy-first Street. Looters were pouring into the store and stumbling out. A police cruiser drove up to the scene and immediately was barraged by flying chunks of cement bricks and empty liquor bottles.

❀   ❀   ❀

The following is how the Rodney King drama developed, what obsessed the good citizens and day-players living in movie-of-the-week land for an entire year, how the script played out, where the car chase took place, and who performed the stunts.

At about twelve-thirty a.m., Sunday, March 3, 1991, Tim and Melanie Singer, a husband-and-wife California Highway Patrol team, were traveling west towards Simi Valley, patrolling the

Foothill Freeway north of Los Angeles. Melanie Singer, who was driving, had exited to an off-ramp when she looked in her rearview mirror and noticed the headlights of a car speeding recklessly. She immediately returned to the freeway and followed the white 1988 Hyundai Excel. A seven-point-eight mile chase ensued with speeds reaching one hundred fifteen miles per hour.

Finally, the Hyundai exited off the freeway and was forced to stop because the driver of a pickup truck heard sirens and pulled over, inadvertently blocking the Hyundai near the entrance of Hansen Dam Park at Foothill and Osborne. A police helicopter and additional cruisers converged on the scene. The first to arrive were Officers Laurence Powell, Timothy Wind, Theodore Briseno, and Sergeant Stacey Koon—all future "defendants" of the beating. The officers drew their guns and crouched behind their cruiser's doors.

Tim Singer shouted for the driver and two black passengers in the Hyundai to get out. Rodney King, the driver, stayed where he was while the passengers obeyed, exited the car, and lay face down on the ground. Melanie Singer ordered King again to get out of the car. King withdrew himself from the car and put his hands on the roof as instructed by Singer. He then looked up at the helicopter, waved, did a little dance, then got on all fours like a dog and began to talk gibberish.

Officers told King to lie down and put his hands behind his back, but instead, he assumed a runner's "on your mark, get set," position. Koon reached for his Taser—an electric stun gun that fires darts containing fifty thousand volts of low amperage electricity—but held off shooting it. Koon, being the ranking officer in charge, ordered the other officers to holster their weapons. He then instructed Briseno, Powell, Wind, and another officer to move in and surround King. By this time there were close to twenty-five LAPD officers on hand. Koon repeatedly ordered King to, "Get your face down!"

It was becoming apparent to Koon and the others King's bizarre behavior may have been due to the fact that he was "dusted"—under the influence of PCP (phencyclidine), an anesthetic and hallucinogen. All the signs were there: he was sweating profusely, talking nonsensically, and his eyes were glazed. Also, PCP users are violent and able to exhibit superhuman strength.

With Taser in hand, Koon gave the command to the four officers to "swarm" King and to jump on top of him. King, in return, tossed off Powell and Briseno from his back. Koon then ordered everyone to stand back and shouted again to King to lie face down on the ground. When King did not obey, Koon fired the Taser gun. King fell to his knees, made a groaning sound, and then lifted himself up, staring at Koon. Koon fired the Taser again. King fell to his right elbow, groaned once more, and again rose to his feet. Koon couldn't believe King was able to survive the Taser.

It was at this point that George William Holliday, a manager of a plumbing company, who had already been awake due to the patter of the police helicopter and wail of sirens, walked onto his second floor bedroom balcony overlooking Foothill Boulevard and Osborne street, and began shooting with a Sony video camera what became the infamous "beating of Rodney King."

King charged like an angry dog towards Powell. Powell drew his baton to defend himself. He struck King wildly, knocking him down. Wind joined in. Briseno contributed by kicking King repeatedly. Koon kept shouting for King to lie face down and to spread his legs and arms out. But King kept trying to rise as the officers' batons were hitting him. For eighty-one seconds King was beaten as he tried to get up. Finally, King cried out, "Please stop."

Briseno cuffed King's hands behind his back; he was double-cuffed and hog-tied (his legs were tied to his hands). An ambulance arrived. King's injuries included multiple fractures, abrasions and bruises, lacerations on his head, a broken cheekbone, and a fracture of the distal fibula in the right leg.

On March 6, King was released from Los Angeles County Men's Central Jail after District Attorney Ira Reiner found insufficient evidence to prosecute him. No traces of PCP were found in King's blood, but he indeed had been drinking because his blood alcohol level was 0.19 at the time of the arrest. The next day, Chief of Police

Daryl Gates announced that Koon, Powell, Wind, and Briseno would be prosecuted.

Holliday's videotape of the King beating played incessantly on L.A.'s television stations for a year. Radio stations and all the newspapers stayed up to date with the status of the accused officers involved with the beating. *The People of the State of California v. Laurence Powell et al.* trial was held in a Simi Valley courtroom because Joan Dempsey Klein, presiding Justice of the Second District of the California Court of Appeal, thought moving the trial to a venue outside of Los Angeles would give the defendants a "fair" trial. The appointed judge, Judge Stanley Weisberg, placed the trial in neighboring Ventura County—in the community of Simi Valley—only about fifteen miles from where the beating had taken place. Virtually no blacks lived there. In stark contrast to South Central, Simi Valley has the lowest crime rate in the nation. Thousands of L.A.'s eighty-three hundred members of the Los Angeles police force lived in Ventura County. And, it is believed that the judge actually chose Simi Valley as the trial's location because he lived in Simi Valley. The residents of Simi Valley watch the same news stations, listen to the same radio broadcasts, and read the same newspapers as the citizens of Los Angeles. So how could holding the trial in Simi Valley increase the "fairness" of the trial?

Out of a jury pool of two hundred sixty people, six were black—none were chosen. The jury included three members of the National Rifle Association and two former military police officers. The jury was seated on March 2, 1992, one day short of a year to the King beating.

One year and fifty-seven days after Rodney King had been beaten and arrested by Los Angeles Police Department officers in Lake View Terrace northwest of downtown Los Angeles, the four white officers accused with the pulverization – Seargeant Koon, Wind, Powell, and Briseno – were acquitted of all charges. The black community of South Central Los Angeles did not agree with the result of the verdict. Their own verdict resulted in looting, gunfire, fifty-five deaths, two thousand three hundred twenty-eight injuries, the burning of eight hundred sixty-two buildings, and property loss exceeding one billion dollars.

❁　　❁　　❁

Craig blew out a long slow whistle. Harold wore a wry smile. Ed shook his head. A few of the low maintenance regulars were in attendance as well as a few extras. Other than them, no one else of any consequence was in the bar, so I was able to pay attention to what was being reported live on the television.

Using the remote, I clicked between all the local news stations. Each had its own helicopter hovering above Florence Avenue and Normandy Boulevard where all the action was taking place. Even though this is one of the most dangerous neighborhoods in the world, it is an area frequented by a lot of people who don't live there. The Los Angeles Coliseum where many sporting events are held is only a few blocks away, as is the University of Southern California.

"Where are the cops?" Craig asked to no one in particular.

He was right. No police were to be found anywhere.

"Jerking off," was Harold's reply.

Windows of cars and storefronts were being smashed. Cars rolled down the street on fire. Concrete bus benches were destroyed to use chunks of concrete for throwing. A black man was standing on the hood of a car smacking the windshield with a two-by-four piece of wood. Glass and debris covered the intersection. The one police car that had been at the looting sight was gone.

The regular cast members strolled into the bar. Bones carried his personal cue for tournament night. Gary also walked in and up to the bar next to Craig. Seeing Craig, Gary, Ed, and Harold together—all veterans of wars—made me realize that what was happening only a few miles away was beginning to look like a war zone.

"Pretty crazy, huh?" Gary said wild-eyed, as I handed him his usual Jack 'n' Coke. Craig just looked at him and then turned his attention back to the TV screen. Bones never talked. He walked over to the pool table and was joined by Gary. They played a game of pool.

The local news was replaced by the network national news. The top story of the day was the acquittal and the riots. Live feed of the riot at Florence and Normandy was carried intermittently by the networks. It was starting to get a little busier at the bar, so I couldn't concentrate on watching TV all night. However, I only had seven players to enter into the games. I conducted the tournament anyway. Gary won thirty-five dollars.

Throughout the night I monitored the riots. The situation in South Central had worsened. Just about the time Bones had smashed the cue ball into the tight rack of billiard balls to begin the tournament, a truck driver named Reginald Denny was himself getting his face smashed. Apparently, Denny drove his eighteen-wheel truck, loaded with twenty-seven tons of sand, unknowingly into the war zone. Rocks went flying through his window. Someone had opened the driver side door and pulled him out into the street. He was held down and kicked. The looter wearing the Malcolm X T-shirt then proceeded to hit Denny three times with a claw hammer. A slab of concrete was also laid into his head by another assailant who knocked Denny unconscious. The man danced a "touchdown pass" dance over Denny's body and another rioter rifled his pockets.

It would be unfair to say that all Afro-Americans in South Central contributed to the looting and the rioting. Reginald Denny was rescued by four black strangers who had been watching the near-killing live on television. From only a few miles away, they jumped into a car, drove to the scene, put Denny in their car, and drove him to Daniel Freeman Memorial Hospital. By the time the rioters were finished with Denny his skull was fractured in ninety-one places. His left eye was dislocated. When Denny arrived at the hospital, he had a seizure. He survived.

Fires were set. Smoke filled the air over South Central. People were running through the streets. Calamity and chaos were everywhere within thirty square miles of the now infamous intersection. Anyone who was white, Korean, or Hispanic became a victim simply by being in the wrong place at the wrong time.

Police were nowhere in sight. It wasn't until much later that a full-blown investigation concluded that police stayed away was because they were not prepared, were overwhelmed, and communication between the command post and other LAPD units was poor. At Parker Center, where LAPD Headquarters is located in downtown L.A., a peaceful crowd protesting the jury's verdict raged out of control. A guard shack at the entrance of the Center's north parking lot was pushed over and set on fire. Protesters fanned out and vandalized government buildings, a hotel, and the *Los Angeles Times* building.

Fires were raging throughout South Central. Arsonists tossing Molotov cocktails were to blame. I flipped through the pages of the *Mr. Boston Official Bartender's Guide* we kept behind the bar to see if a "Molotov Cocktail" had ever been invented. You'd think that a bartender somewhere would have thought of the "Molotov Cocktail" as a great idea—but no one had—*officially* that is. So, in commemoration of the burning down of L.A., I invented the "Molotov Cocktail." This consists of a shot glass three-quarters-filled with Bacardi's Black Rum and a floater of 151 Bacardi's Rum. Bacardi's 151 is flammable. It is to be ignited, and after the flame burns out, swallowed in one gulp. The "Molotov Cocktail" caught on like wildfire. I sold a lot of those.

Firefighters became the new targets. At Martin Luther King Boulevard and Coliseum Street a mob of three hundred pelted the firefighters with concrete and bottles. At eight o'clock, SWAT teams were called in to rescue and protect the firefighters. By ten o'clock, forty-five fires were ablaze across a hundred and five square miles of South Central. At eleven o'clock, one hundred twenty-two fire companies were dowsing flames in South Central. Out of curiosity, I stepped outside onto the sidewalk to look up into the sky. A putrid smell was in the air; sulfur, an acrid odor of burnt metal and wood and asbestos had now clung and mixed into the already low-hanging smog that gripped the city every day.

By now the bar was filled, but not as it usually would have been this time of night. People strolled into the bar either not caring or not knowing what was going on.

Governor Pete Wilson, while in Sacramento, declared Los Angeles to be in a state of emergency. The National Guard was ordered to be mobilized.

I got a call from Dottie at eleven-fifteen.

"Mickey, how's business?"

"A little slower than usual, but business as usual," I answered her.

"I think you better close early tonight."

What was happening only sixteen miles away was beginning to have its effects in the San Fernando Valley.

After I closed the bar, a few of us milled around in the rear parking lot. Others went in search of bars that remained opened. Most went home. Marijuana, cocaine, and beer were passed around. I sat on top of the trunk of my car and smoked a joint with Peter.

7

The next day the riot worsened. Mayor Tom Bradley declared a citywide sunset-to-sunrise curfew beginning that night. I called Dottie and asked her if she was going to keep the bar open. She told me she was going to close the bar at eight o'clock and that I shouldn't bother coming in if I didn't want to. Karen would work the extra two hours.

As soon as I hung up the phone with Dottie the phone rang. Jules wanted to take a ride to see how close we could get to the riots.

"Why would I want to do that?" I asked her.

"Something to do."

"Why don't you look for a job?"

"Do you have anything?"

"I just woke up."

"Call Bones."

"Is that why you're calling me? Let me guess, you have no money, K Dog isn't around because he's setting fires, and you want me to get you high."

"Fuck you."

"Wait in line."

"That's funny. I've got my own line. I can fuck whoever I want."

"Then go ahead, leave me alone." I slammed down the phone's handset. We were acting like kids and I hated her for it.

The intention of a "one night stand" turned into a relationship going on two weeks. What kind of relationship it was and where it was going was beyond me. Every time I vowed to myself not to see her again I thought about the sex. It was always about the sex.

I called her back but her line was busy.

❀　　❀　　❀

Bill answered the door.

"Is she here?" I asked.

"She's sleeping. She's feeling fucked up because you hung up on her this morning."

"Jules has feelings?"

"Yeah, imagine that," Bill confirmed.

I walked softly into Jules's bedroom. The sun was going down. The window shades were drawn. The smoke and soot from the fires, mixed with the smog from an unsettling L.A., ventilated an early eerie darkness through the horizontal slits sifting through the blinds. Jules was sound asleep under the covers wearing a Metallica T-shirt. I stood over her and watched her slowly breathe. They were long breaths. She looked secure in a fetal position, arm over arm with one hand close to her mouth. Innocuous. If she had extended her thumb, she would be sucking it. What visions was she dreaming? Dreams of hope? Wanting? The acceptance of love? I heard her mumble. She was talking in her sleep. She did that occasionally.

"Jules?" I whispered.

She mumbled again, something indistinguishable.

I drew closer to her and knelt on one knee in front of her; my face was eye level with hers. I breathed in.

"Jules, it's Mickey," I whispered again, softly. I considered leaving and letting her sleep but instead I was curious to see if she'd answered me while she was sleeping. I read somewhere that you could do that with a person who talks in their sleep. I didn't believe it, but I tried anyway.

"I'm sorry I hung up on you," I whispered a little louder this time. She moaned faintly.

"Do you know who this is?" I asked, surprised that she responded.

"Mick…" she plainly stated, and when she did, I wanted to be the best friend she could ever have.

Jules shifted slightly. She slowly fluttered her eyes open and looked into my eyes. She awakened as though she was expecting to see me there, as if I had already been there with her when she had fallen asleep, as if her dream had dissolved into reality and it was the most natural thing for me to be next to her.

"Take your clothes off and get in here," she ordered me.

I climbed into her bed. She was wearing nothing but the T-shirt. We made love and then took naps.

When we awoke it was dark.

I warmed up two pizzas I had brought over. I gave one pizza to Bill and asked him not to disturb us for anything. He said he was going out anyway.

"What about the curfew?" I asked Bill.

"What curfew?"

The curfew didn't mean anything. People went out anyway.

"I'm glad we're doing this," Jules said into her third slice of pizza.

"When was the last time you ate?"

"Yesterday."

"You talk in your sleep, you know that."

"I know. What'd I say?"

"You said you loved me."

"I *did not.*"

We laughed.

"You said my name," I told her.

"No, I didn't."

"You were just pretending to be asleep, weren't you?"

She laughed again, and punched my upper arm playfully. We were having a good time together just hanging out sans substances. I got up and turned on the brand new Panasonic twelve-inch TV sitting on top of her cluttered dresser.

We watched the update of the riots. The National Guard had just been deployed. Again, live coverage was taking place from helicopters. Fires were burning everywhere now. Rioters had moved peripherally outside of South Central. They were approaching Hollywood and reports of occasional incidents in the Valley were coming in.

I became bored with L.A. destroying itself, so I started playing with Jules's clit. She stroked my cock.

"Pump me, Mickey."

I turned Jules over and sodomized her. "Harder," she said. The bed was jumping up and down and knocking against the wall.

"Ooww" she moaned.

"Do you want me to stop?"

"No, don't stop, I want it all the way..."

This went on for about ten minutes. I shot my load and then I was out of her. I collapsed on the bed and took off the condom I was wearing. Sweat was pouring out of me. Jules stumbled into the bathroom and returned with a small towel. It was wet and warm. She cleaned me.

"I want you to come again," she said.

"I just *did*."

She swallowed me whole. I started to laugh. It tickled.

"Hit me, Mickey."

"No, I'm not going to hit you." She then whacked me across the face with all her little might and laughed wickedly.

"Why you fucking bitch," I said.

"Yeah, Mickey, hit me."

I pinned her down on the bed and straddled on top of her. I held her wrists down. She lifted her chin, wiggled her tongue out, and laughed.

"Whatta ya goin' to do to me, Mickey? Your dick is too limp to fuck me. Whatta ya gonna do?"

I spit and drooled saliva on her tits. She liked that.

I reached over on the floor to a pile of her clothes and grabbed a pair of white hosiery. I tore the hosiery up the crotch in two, twisted and tied one sheer leg around her right wrist, and then I tied the other end around a rail of the imitation-brass headboard.

She feigned resistance and didn't stop me. "What are you doing to me?"

I then did the same with the other leg of the hosiery and wrist and rail.

She breathed heavy and again faked resistance. "Don't… oh, no…"

I jumped off her. She squirmed.

I found a leather belt in the closet. I looped the belt around her ankle and slipped the end through the buckle part. I then grasped the end of the belt and twisted it around my right hand. I lifted and controlled her leg by using the belt like a puppeteer controls a marionette. My tongue went down on her while grasping the belt and moving her leg wide and high in the air.

She moaned with great pleasure.

After I got tired of sucking her I went into the closet to see what else I could find. There was a man's tie and a long red silk scarf. I tied her ankles to the legs at the foot of the bed.

"You bastard," she said, but she enjoyed what I was doing.

I used a dark blue sashay to blindfold her eyes.

"Eww. Nice touch, lover… can't wait to see what you're going to do next."

"Where's your vibrator?"

"In the bottom drawer."

I opened the bottom drawer, found her vibrator, clicked the switch and slowly and gently rubbed the imitation cock against her clitoris.

"I love you, Mickey."

I untied her left wrist.

"Here, you do it."

I watched Jules work her vibrator, tied up and blindfolded. She threw the vibrator across the room, slamming it against the wall. The batteries came tumbling, tumbling out.

She laughed. "What'd I hit?"

"Nothing, the wall."

She then started playing with herself, moaning and fingering herself the way she knew she liked it best. I sat at the foot of the bed between her spread legs and watched.

After Jules finished masturbating and coming to orgasm, I handcuffed both her wrists to the rail up and behind her head. I then went into the living room to have a cigarette. I think I fell asleep.

❀   ❀   ❀

"So, do we stop seeing other people or not?" Jules asked, spread-eagled on the bed as I uncuffed and untied her.

"You mean *you* want a commitment?"

"Don't you want me exclusively for your own?"

I feared such a proposition. I knew deep down in my heart it would never work with Jules. "I can't tame you, I don't think you want to be tamed. You won't be able to do it."

"You tamed me tonight," she said with a wicked smile, "I could be yours forever with sex like that."

"Sex? Fucking? Making love? Which is it?"

"Which is it to you?"

I thought about it. I was too confused by my own question to answer.

"Sex is on top," Jules said.

"Remember the first time we met and you called me from your 'boyfriend's' house, from the bathroom?" I asked her.

"I know that's always bothered you."

"Well, I mean, you do that sort of thing, and what am I supposed to think? How can I trust you?"

"He was nobody, Mickey. Just somebody I was fucking."

"Am I just somebody you're fucking?"

Jules got angry. "Forget it! Just forget the whole thing." She got up and lit a cigarette. "Let's get some coke."

"No."

"Yeah."

"I said 'no'."

"Suit yourself. I'm getting some."

Jules started to get dressed. Without bothering to put on panties, she slipped on a flared red miniskirt—no shower, the scent of sex oozing out of her pores.

"Where you going?" I asked.

"Out," Jules said as she reached for a black leather Versace brassiere.

"Make sure it's good stuff."

"You said you didn't want any. So you're not getting any."

"After all the times I turned you on?"

She didn't say anything. She quickly rummaged through a drawer full of jewelry.

"Bitch." I stood up. "You fucking bitch!"

"Fuck off," Jules said while wrapping a string of white pearls around her neck.

I started to get dressed myself while I watched Jules put on dangling pearl earrings that matched the necklace. "I can't believe you," I said.

She was giving me the silent treatment now and proceeded to apply makeup to her face. She started with eye shadow. A sick feeling ached in my stomach.

"After what we just did, you're just gonna get up and leave. Didn't that mean anything to you?"

"It's just sex. I can get that anytime, anywhere."

"Well *I'm* leaving," I said.

"See ya."

"Fuck you."

"What was it that you said to me this morning? Oh yeah, wait in line."

I pulled up my boots. "Where you going?" I finally got it out, "Gonna go shoot somebody again?"

Jules stopped applying her makeup and looked at me unimpressed. "What took you so long? I thought you were never gonna mention it." She turned back to the mirror and worked her face.

"You knew I saw you?"

"When I pulled out onto Sepluveda after I shot Jimi, I saw your car."

"What happened to him?"

"He's fine, the little crook."

"You could have killed him."

"I aimed low. I shot him in the foot. I was aiming for his balls."

"What about the shot in the house?"

"I missed, and what the fuck were you doing following me?"

"I was on the way to your house and saw you make the turn at Sepulveda and Victory. So I followed you."

Jules said nothing, applying red lipstick to her swollen sexed lips.

"What about this guy, Jimi?" I asked.

"What about him?"

"He the guy who called you, said he was going to kill you?"

"Who knows?"

"Does he know where you live?"

"Of course not. You'd think I'd shoot at somebody who knew where I lived?" She stopped what she was doing and turned to me. "Did you take my gun?"

"No."

She went back to her lips. "Somebody did."

"How'd you get into my apartment that night?"

Jules reached over on the other side of the dresser for her keys. She took one key off the ring and tossed it to me. "I had a copy made when I kept your car. I was going to go to your apartment while you were working and rip you off that night."

"Why didn't you?"

"I guess I *liked* you… better take the key."

She rummaged through her closet and slipped into a pair of black sling-back pumps. She looked like the slut she was. "I gotta go."

"Look—"

"No, you look. I'm like a tiger in this cage. I need to get out and prowl. I need to get outta here. And, you're right, you *can't* tame me."

The beauty of her sleeping turned into a nightmare.

Thursday had been the worst day of the riots. The National Guard was very slow and too late moving out. There seemed to have been a snafu in the organization of their deployment. On Friday, Rodney King, fighting back tears, made a live statement on television. "People, I just want to say, can we all get along? Can we all get along? Can we stop making it horrible for the older people and the kids?" He felt bad and to blame for the riots.

Dottie kept the bar open throughout the weekend because the riots seemed to have been contained to the "other side of the hill"; however, business was slow. At the same time I made the left on Van Nuys Boulevard to drive home Friday night/early Saturday morning after locking up the bar, the first detachment of thirty-five hundred soldiers and Marines were on their way from Fort Ord in Northern California down to Los Angeles.

By Sunday, there were a combined total of thirteen thousand Guards, Federal troops, and LAPD officers on the streets.

Early Monday evening, May 4, Mayor Bradley lifted the curfew. The riots were officially over.

8

I felt the urge to start writing again. I'd been working on a half-dozen screenplays in various forms of development. Some were completed, half-completed, outlined, others had a long way to go. One story in particular I was working on is entitled "Restless Summer," and is based on my life while living in New York City during the late seventies and early eighties. It hadn't been easy to write. I'd pick up the script many times and put it away just as many. Pain and bad memories. I'm not proud of the things I did—just the same way I'm not proud about some of the things I'd done in La-La-Land.

I grew up in Port Chester, New York, a suburb near the Connecticut border less than thirty minutes outside of Manhattan. Purely upper-middle-class. My dad commuted by train into Manhattan. He worked as a copy editor for the *Daily News*, earned promotion to senior copy editor, now retired. My mother taught third grade. Still does.

I have an older brother, Tim. Tim is a successful contractor who specializes in international low-income family housing. He keeps an apartment on the Upper West Side of Manhattan but is usually traveling all over the world on business. The last time I heard he was in Singapore.

After I turned sixteen, I was awarded the privilege to drive. My dad let me borrow the car on a Saturday night. Actually, it was my mom's Buick Skylark. They both thought I was just taking a girlfriend out to the movies or grabbing a few burgers at the local McDonald's and hanging out with my high school friends. We drove into Manhattan instead. We could have taken the train, but it was easier passing a joint and a Seagram bottle in the car.

In 1976, I graduated from Port Chester High School and turned eighteen. My friends and I were already getting in to bars. It was the Bicentennial year and we found America's two hundredth birthday certain cause for celebration. Then again, any excuse was cause enough to get rip-roaring drunk.

For the next year I worked as a dishwasher and busboy at Nuzzio's, an Italian restaurant in nearby White Plains. The busboys, including myself, would drink the left-over bottles of wine and what was left over in glasses. I sideswiped my mom's Skylark against a guardrail on the way home one night and sped off before any police arrived. My parents thought it was time to think seriously of a career.

I enrolled at New York University. My grades in high school were above average. I enjoyed reading and learning came easy to me. English and literature were my favorite subjects. Raymond Chandler was my favorite author. I love movies. I especially like Humphrey Bogart, and the films of the forties and fifties intrigue me. I entered NYU's motion picture production program, lived in Greenwich Village, and worked part-time as a waiter at McSorley's, the famous beer joint and saloon.

At that time the disco era was in its heyday. Studio 54 was in its drug-induced glory. Unfortunately, moving into the City turned out to not be such a good idea. The nightlife became my downfall. And I owe the fault of that decadence in part to Gus Scarletti and Ritchie Salento.

I met Gus at NYU. He grew up on Grand Concourse in the upper Bronx—a tough neighborhood. We had the same interests: movies, girls, and getting stoned. Gus was Italian and good-looking. He had a way with women I have never seen any other man have. His women were always gorgeous, slender, and sexy.

Gus's talent was hot-wiring automobiles. On a Friday night he would "borrow" a car he'd find parked on a nearby street and on

Sunday night he'd return the car and park it on the same block where he'd found it. Gus was a barbiturate addict who introduced me to the world of seconals, tuinals, nebutals; any pharmaceutical with an "al" at the end of it.

I met Ritchie through Gus. Ritchie was strikingly handsome, dark, tall, and well built. His parents were originally from Sicily. Both were dead. Ritchie had been living on his own since he was twenty years old in Forest Hills, Queens, New York. He'd never been out of the City in his entire life. He worked the third rail in the tunnels underneath Grand Central Station. He joked how he would have lunch with the rats. Ritchie was six years older than me and Gus and a weekend heroin addict.

The three of us were notorious together. It was the same scenario every weekend. Gus and Ritchie would meet at my apartment near Washington Square Park late Friday night, wait for the drugs to kick in, and then we'd hit the discos. We had no trouble finding our way in between the legs of beautiful women. At times we shared our women. They were a wholesome commodity.

It was the adventures of these weekends with which I began formulating a screenplay. There were plenty of *mis*adventures and music to make an exciting film and soundtrack. I didn't need to embellish too much. I changed the names of the characters to protect the guilty. NICK plays Gus, TONY is Ritchie, and my character's name is JOEY. The screenplay is about the search for fulfillment and identity. In "scriptdom" parlance it's a "coming-of-age" story. Only the protagonist—myself—survives the turmoils of disillusionment after learning his lesson the hard way. *Everybody dance, clap your hands, clap your hands.*

In one scene, Nick steals a Volkswagen, picks up Joey, and they drive out to the Hamptons for some weekend summer fun. But they don't make it because Nick is so downed out that he falls asleep at the wheel on the Long Island Expressway and crashes the car. They run from the scene and escape by hopping aboard the No.7 Flushing local back to Manhattan. Joey is bleeding from the nose and admits himself into St. Vincent's Hospital the next day with a broken nose and lies to the doctors about how he got mugged by two teenagers who came up to him and asked him for a cigarette. A surgeon fixes Joey's nose and gives him a prescription for Percodan, which he of course abuses. Nick barely got a scratch.

In another scene, Nick and Joey are sitting on a fire escape early in the morning after a night of nightclubbing. Nick had just shot someone. Joey didn't know Nick had a gun. We learn about their disillusionment of living in the city.

EXTERIOR—TONY'S APARTMENT/FIRE ESCAPE—DAY

Joey and Nick are sitting on the fire escape outside the window of Tony's apartment. They smoke cigarettes and watch the PEDESTRIANS below. Tony is inside sleeping off a hangover from the night before.

                    NICK
He got what he deserved.

                    JOEY
Nick, you don't go around shooting some guy you
never met outside a nightclub on a dark street just
because the guy's jealous over you and his
girlfriend. That's his problem.

                    NICK
You think I killed him?

                    JOEY
No. It looked like you grazed him. I saw him reach
for his upper arm.

                    NICK
What if I killed him?

JOEY

You didn't kill him, so stop worrying about it. It's
just a good thing we got out of there when we did.

NICK

You think the cops will find me?

JOEY

The guy doesn't know who you are. You were just
some other guy talking to his girl.

NICK

Yeah, she was a knock-out, eh? She was gonna give
me her number before her boyfriend showed up.
We got out of there fast, eh, Joey?

JOEY

I didn't know you had a gun, Nick. Why didn't you
tell me you were strapped? Where'd you get the
fuckin' gun?

NICK

I'm holding it for Vinnie while he's in jail.

JOEY

Your brother. Figures. That's just fuckin' great.
        (beat)
What's going to happen to him?

NICK

I don't know. Bail is too high. My ma and I, we
can't raise that much money.

JOEY

Maybe he'll get off on an insanity plea.
    (scoffs)
God knows his wife drove him crazy.

NICK

She's no good, Joey. But I couldn't tell Vinnie that.
I didn't want to hurt him. I knew if he found out
he'd o' killed her.
    (beat—reflects)
She was cheating on him left and right.

JOEY

How do you know?

NICK

Pedro's seen her.

JOEY

You're gonna believe that low-life?

NICK

Other people too. Other people, they'd tell me, not
Vinnie, they'd tell me. I didn't know what to do.
They got no reason to lie to me.

JOEY

Everybody lies, what's the difference?

NICK

    (getting angry)
Hey, what the fuck do you know? I'm still up in the
fuckin' Bronx, remember? Remember? The hood
we *both* grew up in? You don't know what's goin'
on.

JOEY

I know enough. That's why I got out of there.

NICK

Well, lucky you.

JOEY

All right, all right.
(beat)
How'd Vinnie find out the baby wasn't his?

NICK

He came home early from work one day and heard
her talking on the phone to the real father. ...the
real father from two years ago. And she was still
making him.

JOEY
(shaking his head)
God...

NICK

He went crazy, Joey. He went crazy. (tears coming
to Nick's eyes) That's why he went nuts. He went
nuts, Joey. He threw the kid out the second-floor
window. The second-floor window, Joey!

Joey stands up and looks down at the sidewalk, imagining what it
would be like for a two-year-old baby to be thrown from a window.
He flips his cigarette butt and watches it fall to the ground.

JOEY

You know, you hear about this stuff all the time, in
the papers, on TV... you don't think it's gonna
happen to you though...

NICK

He went over the edge, Joey. He knows he done
wrong…
          (wipes a tear away)
…at least the kid's okay.
          (beat)
What are we gonna do, Joey?

JOEY

'Bout what?

NICK

Us. You, me, Tony, my brother, I've had it with this
city… it's choking me. I've lived my whole life
here, never been anywhere else… like to know
what Florida's like, California even… fuck, I ain't
even never been to Disneyland.

JOEY

Disneyland? Who the fuck cares about Disneyland.

NICK

We're losers, Joey, we're nothin' but a bunch of
losers.

JOEY

          (looks at Nick)
Don't talk that way. We'll do something. We'll do
something big. You and me and Tony, I got this
plan, see…

NICK

What kind o' plan?

                    JOEY
I been thinkin' 'bout somethin' for a long time how
we can get out o' here...

                    NICK
Like about what?

                    JOEY
Like about what? Like about thirty grand. That's
what. I got a plan...

CUT TO:

LONG SHOT from POV of STREET of Joey and Nick on the fire
escape. We don't hear Joey, but we can see he's very excited about
something and explaining it to Nick.

                ❊   ❊   ❊

   Yeah, those were the good old days. Except in real life Gus
disappeared one night. Ritchie and I never saw him again. *Good
times. Leave your past behind.*
   After Gus's disappearance my studying went down the toilet. I
dropped out of NYU and drove a cab seventy hours a week. After I
got tired of getting robbed and cleaning cum stains and vomit from
the back seat, I found a job as a limousine driver. I still had to clean
cum stains and vomit, but at least the clientele weren't robbing me.
   I switched over to another limo service that had a more
respectable clientele. International Limousine had a major account
with 20th Century Fox. For four years I drove around celebrities and
VIPs. I escorted the best, including Tom Cruise, Michael Douglas,
Cher, Kate Jackson, Tom Hanks, Sally Field, Richard Dreyfuss,
Steve Martin, Arnold Schwarzenegger, Mel Brooks, Barry
Marshack...

Right off the bat, from the first time I picked up Barry Marshack, the director, we developed a casual chauffeur/Hollywood Mogul relationship. And every time he came to New York he requested me to pick him up at the airport—take him to meetings, dinners, the theater, anywhere and everywhere.

I'll never forget the day when I thought all my dreams would come true. I was dropping off Barry at the TWA terminal at JFK.

"So you think you might want to come out to L.A. sometime?" Barry asked me at the curb as I was unloading his luggage from the trunk.

"Hell yeah, I've been wanting to go out there for a long time, see what all the fuss is about."

"Well, maybe when you get a chance," Barry said to me as he reached into his blue blazer and pulled out a TWA ticket envelope, "you can come out and visit. Here." He handed me the envelope.

"What's this?"

"It's your tip."

I peered inside the envelope: an open-date roundtrip ticket to LAX, Los Angeles International Airport.

"Is it okay if I use this one-way?"

❄ ❄ ❄

My limousine boss gave me all the jobs I wanted, and for the next month I saved as much money as I could. I gave notice and withdrew four thousand three hundred forty dollars and fifty-seven cents, closing my account from Chase Manhattan Bank. I asked to borrow another two thousand from my parents. They gave me twenty-five hundred, and I flew to Los Angeles, California.

CUT TO:

LOS ANGELES—ESTABLISHING SHOT

I checked into the Hollywood Motel on Cahuenga Boulevard,

purchased a 1982 Chrysler LeBaron for two thousand dollars, and moved into the Regal Courts two weeks later. I went to visit Barry. He had just wrapped *The Maraschino Kid* and was in post-production editing the film. I worked as a waiter at Acapulco's, a Mexican restaurant across the street from the NBC studios. Working in the restaurant business is a good way to have a flexible schedule and be able to work freelance. I worked on Barry's next motion picture as a production assistant.

For the next four years I continued to work freelance as a grip, production assistant, and sometimes as an assistant-to-the-producer. I purchased a computer and began writing screenplays.

Things were going fine until I started falling into my old habits again. I was getting depressed because things weren't happening fast enough for me. What an idiot.

CUT BACK TO:

INTERIOR—MICK'S APARTMENT—NIGHT

As I sat staring at the next blank page of my script watching news coverage on TV of the aftermath of the riots with the sound turned off, wondering what scene to write next in my New York true-to-life story, I thought about where I had been and where I was going in my life. It was disheartening trying to "make it" in Hollywood. It's dangerous being single, alone, and vulnerable. There are so many ways to fuck up and destroy yourself. My life was turning into a film noir.

I went down to the local Von's, bought a bottle of gin, and continued to stare at the computer screen. I was able to kick out two more scenes. I fell asleep. After I awoke the next day, I printed out what I had written from the night before. The pages weren't too bad. I just needed to keep "plugging away" as the veterans say.

CUT TO:

EXTERIOR—McDEE'S COCKTAIL LOUNGE & BAR/
PARKING LOT—NIGHT

Tuesday night. The soot was settling from the riots. Normally, I didn't like going into McDee's on my night off because I had enough of the place working there and I really didn't want to see the same assholes if I didn't have to. But I went anyway. I put on my Levis, a black T-shirt, and black boots.

I pulled into the rear parking lot with the Mustang and saw Jamie about to enter the rear entrance. She looked good that night wearing tight-fitting faded Calvin Klein blue jeans and an oversized white silk blouse tied into a knot just below her huge tits. She was wearing long slender drop earrings and sculpted-heel dress sandals. She saw me and hesitated before going in. I knew the security monitor's camera range so I drove beyond it and waved to her. She strutted to my side of the car.

"What's going on?" she asked, leaning in and giving me a kiss.

"Got bored at home, thought I'd come down here see what I'm missing."

She scoffed. "Place sucks."

"Wanna go somewhere else?" I asked her.

"Whatta ya have in mind?"

"Does it make a difference?"

"I suppose not. Anywhere's better than here. Where's Jules?" she asked me with a sardonic smile.

"Who knows…"

Jamie's smile widened, she threw her hair back, and looked around.

"Bones in there?" I asked.

"Don't worry, I got stuff." Jamie walked across in front of the Mustang looking at me with her big green eyes and smirking the whole time until she opened the passenger door and got in.

"What's that look for?" I asked.

"Nothing… just drive, baby."

While I drove, Jamie unscrewed an amber vial, tipped some coke into the lid, and placed it under my nose. I took a hit in one nostril. She gave me another hit for my other nostril. Then she took a couple of hits. Jamie didn't freebase and she hated people who did.

"You know a guy named Louie Vicente?" I asked.

"Never heard of him."

"What about a black guy, gang banger, Crip, goes by K Dog."

"Black like a Hershey Kiss? Drives a BMW?"

"Yeah, that's him."

"Seen him once over at Jules's."

"You've been over there?"

"Couple of times. She's a crack head. I stay away from crack heads. You do that shit, Mickey?"

"Why was Jules at Sybil? What she do?"

"A four-eighty-seven-three. Grand theft auto. Her and one of K Dog's homeboys. She's got something going, but I don't know what. You should stay away from her."

"Yeah, that's what everybody keeps telling me."

"Like who?"

"Peter—"

"Him, you can't trust. He's a wimpy motherfucker and a baby."

"Was Jules involved in the car that got stolen from the parking lot?"

"No one knows for sure. She went to Sybil for stealing a car out of the Lion's Den over on Roscoe. She swiped some guy's keys off the bar that had one of those car alarms attached to the key chain. She went outside when he was in the men's room and started pressing the thing until a Porsche chirped. She got in and then got pulled over by a five-o because one of the taillights was out. She gave the cop some story it was her boyfriend's car. They arrested her because she'd been drinking. She blew a point fourteen. While she was in the holding cell a report came in that the Porsche was stolen. That's how she ended up at Sybil."

I turned right and drove south on Lankershim Boulevard. I obeyed the speed limit and kept looking into the rearview mirror.

"I need to get a new life," I admitted.
Jamie smirked. "Right, baby."

INTERIOR—UNIVERSAL CITY BAR & GRILL—LATER

We walked into Universal City Bar & Grill across the street from Universal Studios. Movie stars never went into the place, but a lot of the technicians and secretaries did. They were two to three cuts above the customers who went into McDee's. We were upscaling. The place was clean and well-lit. A blues-jazz combo was performing that night. We sat in the back not far from the pool table.

Jamie had a few of her usual Capecodders. I ordered Margaritas made to my specification: one-and-a-half-ounces of 1800 Cuervo Tequila, half that amount of Grand Marnier, an eighth of an ounce of lime juice, and a deep splash of sour mix and orange juice, shaken and poured, sans salt. We sat and drank and smoked cigarettes and listened to the music. Jamie and I passed the amber vial back and forth to each other and went into the restrooms to take hits. We had to be careful. There were rumors of undercover narcotic agents at Universal. We never had the problem of undercover cops at McDee's. Strange, because McDee's had the reputation for being the biggest drug bar in the Valley. Maybe Bone's was paying them off, too.

Jamie had been living at her older sister's place since she'd gotten divorced a year ago. Her sister, Amy, had a real job working as a legal secretary for a personal injury attorney—as opposed to Jamie, who relied on alimony, child support, and dealing cocaine. Jamie's daughter, Ashley, slept in another room. Jamie's ex-husband took Ashley on alternate weekends. Jamie's sister didn't allow any of Jamie's boyfriends to stay over. In other words she couldn't bring me back to her place and fuck me. We could talk quietly in the living room, but that was it. Why bother? So we went back to my place and fucked. I rammed it up Jamie real hard that night. She, too, liked it in the back door. It was easy gaining entrance. The door was wide open and there was plenty of room.

❀   ❀   ❀

Living paycheck to paycheck, week to week, tips to tips, and night to night sucked. I was never able to save any money. Of course, being addicted to drugs, booze, and women made it all the more difficult. I kept replaying in my mind how I was going to get out of that dilemma. If I could only have sold a screenplay and made a million bucks. Yeah, right. The more I thought about the dubious notion of success, the more I got depressed. The more I got depressed, the more I didn't care. The more I didn't care, the more I would drink and snort and fuck everything in sight. It was an unending vicious cycle and I wanted to slit my throat. But I didn't have the guts.

9

I hadn't seen Jules since the night I tied her up and she got pissed-off at me and me at her and we both essentially walked out on each other, except for Thursday night when she bounced into the bar and I politely informed her that she wasn't allowed in there and that if Dottie found out—which she would—it would be my ass. Jules stormed out, taking Peter in tow.

Another weekend was ahead of me trapped behind the bar as I suddenly felt the undeniable urge to get high as a kite. Somebody gave me a small white pill, calling it a "white cross," telling me it would keep my kite flying for a long time. On top of the crank, cocaine, Irish Mist, and another "white cross," I felt no pain and mixed drinks, flipped open beer bottles, and poured drafts faster than people were asking for them. I proceeded to party with the multitude, flying higher than anyone and never came down for three days and three nights. I was seeing black spots in front of my eyes by Saturday night/slash/Sunday morning. But with a little more help from white rabbits, er, white crosses, I managed.

If I can get this straight this is what I *think* happened that weekend:

I spent all my tip money from Thursday night and bought five vials of coke from Bones. I dragged Jamie home with me—who incidentally was very inebriated—with the intention of raw and kinky sex. Jamie, not waiting for me to close the apartment door, began to strip naked and slipped her robin's-egg blue sundress over

96

her head, beads of pre-sex sweat already pouring off her stumbling body. She kicked off her matching sundress fuck-me pumps, one hitting the TV and the other almost flying out the window. I laid out two long lines of cocaine for us to inhale up our nostrils. I made two stiff Smirnoff screwdrivers, wondering why I didn't feel like I was stoned enough.

Jamie was in the bathroom a little too long.

"Hey, Jamie. Jamie," I said into the six-coated Navajo-white painted wood of the closed bathroom door. "Jamie!"

I opened the door to find Jamie passed out on the floor with a Xanax in her hand. She was on tranquilizers that night. I popped the Xanax in my mouth and swallowed. I picked up Jamie and carried what felt like one hundred and thirty-five pounds to my bed. I spread her legs and sucked her pussy. No response. What a drag.

I cooked up some cocaine. I became incredibly horny and tried to wake Jamie for a little cognizant action. I sucked on her again, hoping the stimulation would revive her. It didn't and only made me feel more frustrated. I thought of putting it into her while she was passed out, spread out for the wanting, but I've tried that before with other women and it just doesn't work. I knew what fucking the dead was like.

I searched for an *L.A. Weekly* I knew I had somewhere in my apartment, found it, turned to the *Adult Services* section and called "Ambrosia." As I expected, I got an answering machine informing me that "Ambrosia" would call me right back. *Between johns,* I thought. I called a few more numbers with similar outgoing messages and left my own messages on all their machines to call Michael ASAP for the services of a "massage." I used my real name because they would check my driver's license when they arrived at my place anyway. I've done this before. I opened the drawer where I kept my finances and counted out two hundred dollars in cash.

The phone rang. I took a hit from the pipe because I liked talking to hookers on the phone when I'm freebased and ecstatic with the possibility of sex with a strange woman.

"Hello?"

"Hi, is this Michael?"

"Yeah, who's this?"

"Ambrosia."

"Hi, Ambrosia."

"What do you want?" she said clean and sober.

"A massage with a hand release."

"Where are you?"

"Sherman Oaks. Where are you?"

"Reseda."

"Okay."

"It's a hundred dollars for thirty minutes or when you ejaculate, whichever comes first."

Whichever cums first.

"Are you alone?" she asked me without pause.

"Well, actually, there's another girl, but she's—"

"Is she going to watch or participate?"

"Probably watch."

"Then it's one-fifty."

I gave Ambrosia the directions to my apartment and a barely attractive girl of about twenty-two with dazzling green eyes and long wild curly-crimped auburn hair, wearing a Claude Montana black leather waist-jacket, black fishnet stockings, and six-inch black leather stiletto heels was at my door. She was blitzed-out make-upped with turquoise eye shadow, false eyelashes, heavy black eyeliner, and cherry red lip-gloss. Imitation diamond earrings dangled halfway to her neck. Her seductive scent was YSL's Opium Secret de Parfum.

As soon as she entered—and they all do this—she walked around the apartment opening closets to see if anyone was hiding and would jump out and strangle her—or whatever they were afraid of. I thought of the girl who came over to my apartment and rifled through my drawers and closets and stole my hairbrush and Trojan lubricated condoms. But this was different.

Ambrosia walked into the bedroom and saw Jamie splayed out on the bed.

"Is she dead?"

"No, she's not dead. She's asleep."

"Asleep or passed out?"

"Both, I guess. What's the difference?"

"This isn't good."

"Look, here's a hundred. You'll be out of here in twenty minutes..."

"One-fifty."

"One-fifty."

"Let me see your driver's license."

I had it in my hand. She looked at it and gave it back to me.

"One-fifty," she repeated.

I gave her the money.

Ambrosia slipped off her jacket, underneath of which was revealed a Jean-Paul Gaultier black leather fetish corset, black wet-look polyvinyl underpants, and a green-to-match-her-eyes garter belt on each thigh. She threw the jacket over the back of my sofa.

"Do you have anything to drink?" she asked me.

I made her a vodka on the rocks, gave her a snort of cocaine, and asked her if she wanted anything else.

"Like what?"

"Well, do—you—smoke—it?"

We had sex for two hours on the sofa, on the living room floor, on a chair, on the sink in the bathroom, against the wall, and in the closet. The closet was her idea. I couldn't get her out of my apartment. Her pager, set on vibrator, danced across my dining room table from one end to the other and finally landed on the floor by the time we were finished and couldn't fuck each other anymore.

Jamie moved.

"Wouldn't it be cool if she never knew what just went on," I said to Ambrosia as she stood naked studying all the phone numbers on her pager.

"I gotta go anyway. It's been fun. No extra charge," Ambrosia said beginning to get dressed. "Call me again," she said as she walked out the door and gently closed it.

Jamie was a bitch when she woke up. It was seven thirty-five a.m. and I was down to my last vial of coke. I turned Jamie on with a good strong line. She looked a mess but came round after the hit. She took a shower. I sat and smoked the last of my cigarettes watching the *Today Show*. I was geeking, guilty, and nervous. I couldn't wait for Jamie to leave so I could pace my apartment and hate myself all day. Except I had to drive Jamie home. We snorted the last of my stash. After all, I kind of owed it to her for fucking another girl practically on top of her.

It wasn't a pleasurable experience driving Jamie home as I absorbed myself with every car behind me, in front of me, on the side of me, approaching me, passing me, and letting general paranoia have its early morning way with me. Everyone was on his or her way to work. I had to keep checking in the rearview mirror that I was wearing my Ray-Bans. Jamie didn't feel like talking, which was fine for me because all I would have been able to babble was "Blahh, blohdi, blahhh." She did ask me though, "Was there someone else in the apartment last night?"

"No, why would there be someone else in the apartment?"

"I thought I heard voices and some kind of banging."

I returned to the Regal safely having only one cop car pass me from the opposite direction and a CHP motorcyclist who scared the hell out of me when he passed me on the left and zoomed ahead on Magnolia Boulevard.

❀   ❀   ❀

On Friday and Saturday nights, McDee's sponsored live music. No cover, no charge. Dottie was a genius. The place was packed both nights. Surprisingly, I felt okay. I hadn't done anything in the way of brain embellishment all day on Friday and didn't do anything until about ten that night when I felt like my kite was going to get *tangled in a tree*. Bones *gave* me two vials—for being such a good customer, I guess. I really didn't need anything else. Jamie was not in that night, so I cruised the room to see if there were any likely candidates for sex later that evening. *What celibacy policy, Dottie? I don't remember us talking about a celibacy policy.* I thought of Jules. I thought of whom she might be getting off with and going down on at that moment.

No girl—or woman—who I wanted was really available. I thought of calling Ambrosia but dismissed the thought because it had occurred to me that it was May 8th and I hadn't yet paid the rent and didn't want to get another phone call from the landlord reminding me that *YOU Mister Michael Collins... your rent is overdue.*

It was closing time. Charlene and I were discussing who we would let stay after hours when someone came running in from the rear door saying there was a fight outside. Both Charlene and I looked immediately up at the security monitor and saw a few onlookers standing in the parking lot and a low-riding Chevy Impala speeding out into the street. We ran outside and discovered that one of the band members was bent over a Marshal amplifier he was in the process of putting inside the band's Dodge van. The band member was bleeding from his head. The gist of the matter was that four Mexicans in the Impala drove up, three jumped out, and ripped off the band member's Fender Stratocaster guitar. He tried to fight them off and got hit across the head with a tire iron. The Mexicans got away with the guitar. No one was able to stop them because it happened so fast, or no one was in the immediate vicinity to help, or to bother to help, or brave enough to help, or sober enough to help, or cognizant to act quickly enough to help. I don't know how it came about that the police arrived, because neither Charlene nor myself called them. We always tried to keep the LAPD as little interested in McDee's as possible. But they were there asking questions. It put a damper on everyone's buzzes, especially since another three squad cars arrived and suddenly the place was crawling with police. I thought of Rodney King.

The band member was rolling around on the ground holding his hands over his head where blood coagulated with long black hair. An ambulance arrived with its siren blaring unnecessarily. The band member tried to get up on his own but was forced down and restrained from doing so by the paramedics. They placed him on the gurney. The other band members consoled him shouting things like, "Hey, dude, you'll get some good drugs now." A Kodak moment.

One of the cops, Miller, according to his badge, asked others and me what happened. "How much did he have to drink?"

"He had a few beers and a couple of shots." I lied about the number of shots.

"A few beers and a few shots," he repeated at the same time he was writing it down.

"No. That's a few beers and a *couple* of shots," I lied again.

"Uh-huh," he said while nodding and writing.

Charlene and I cleaned up the bar as slowly as we could, stalling for time, because two squad cars stayed in the back parking lot opposite each other, talking the way cops talk parked driver side to driver side when there's nothing else to do. Charlene and I stood and stared into the security monitor. It was almost four o'clock and way past the time we should have been out of there.

"When are they going to leave?" I said. I was paranoid because I knew if they pulled me over after I drove out of McDee's I'd definitely win a "Driving Under the Influence" arrest. I'd received one DUI already on the Hollywood Freeway after coming home from a night of free lambada lessons at some Latino bar called "Diego's" near McArthur Park. Another DUI would mean more time in jail and at least a year without a license. I did not want that to happen.

"Here, do a hit," Charlene offered.

"Are you out of your mind?"

Charlene laughed.

Finally, the cops left but I was still paranoid. Charlene said she wasn't sticking around to baby sit me and walked out to her Dodge Charger and drove away. I stood there in the middle of McDee's like an idiot not knowing what to do. I paced for five minutes, lit a cigarette, practiced pool shots, then I said the hell with it and took a chance and made my way home. I let out a genuine sigh of relief when the gates of the Regal Court's parking garage opened and I drove in.

Once in my apartment I didn't know what to do with myself. The sun would be sneaking into my windows any minute. I took out another screenplay I was working on and thought about writing. That didn't work. I had nothing to drink and had no drugs—not even one lousy Excedrin P.M., no NyQuil—nothing to help me unwind. I lay down on the bed and stared at the ceiling. I jerked off and somehow managed to fall asleep. The phone rang. It was Peter. He had been up all night and was coming over with "some good shit."

Peter's shit was Colombian. I didn't want to smoke weed because it would have really made me fucked up wired. It was five in the fucking morning. "No," I said.

"Where's Jules been?" he asked while deseeding grass.

"How should I know?"

"I thought you were going out with her."

"I don't know what I'm doing anymore."

"Dude, get your life together, man."

"You were with her Thursday night. She yanked you out with her after I had to throw her out."

"Dottie still won't let her in, huh?"

"No. And I'm not sure I'd want her in there anyway."

"She's bad news."

Peter rolled a perfect joint. He licked the gummed edge with his tongue and looked at it admiringly.

"Where'd you guys go?" I asked.

"When?"

"*Thursday night.*"

"Back to her place." He then lit the joint and inhaled so deeply that a third of the joint was ash now. Peter held his breath while I just stared at him. Then he let out a cloud of smoke. "Want some?"

"I said, 'no.'"

Peter looked at the joint like it was some piece of fucking art and then took another hit. "Got anything to drink?"

"Water."

The apartment was now filled with the sweet aroma of marijuana.

"I'll go get something when the stores open," he offered.

"I can't spend any money."

"That's okay, man, I'm buying. You've bought me plenty of drinks."

"Dottie did. I didn't. Those drinks that I *buy* you and everybody else come from Dottie. Don't ever fucking forget that."

"Eww. How noble."

I didn't say anything. I was depressed. Finally I said, "Jules is a few sandwiches short of a picnic, you know that?"

Peter snickered. "I tried to warn you, buddy."

"Hmmm."

"She'll bleed you to death. But you like that, don't you, motherfucker?"

"What? What do I like?"

"This whole self-destructive bullshit."

"And you're Tony Robbins."

"Hey, all I do is smoke a little grass now and then."

This time *I* snickered. "Not to mention selling the stuff to high schoolers."

"Well…" his voice trailing off…

"Did she tell you I almost tried to strangle her?"

"You *did* strangle her."

"Bitch."

"She's bad, man. She'll take both our dicks at the same time and suck the bones dry anywhere anytime. And I mean 'anywhere' and 'anytime'."

"Like the Laundromat?"

"What Laundromat?"

"Gary said she gave some guy a blow job in a Laundromat."

Peter burst out laughing. "That's a good one. I hadn't heard that, but I wouldn't put it past her."

Peter snickered and smoked carefully so he wouldn't inhale and gulp the tiny roach he was now holding burning at the end of his fingertips. "She likes you, man. She told me so."

"I feel privileged."

"You have to understand something, man," Peter continued,

"you're never going to be happy with her, so don't even go down that dark fucking alley. You're never gonna change her, she's always gonna be the same conniving liar freebasing whore she'll always be. You don't need that shit."

"Jeez, who'd think a little girl from Kansas City could be so much trouble."

"Kansas City?"

"Yeah, Kansas City."

"Jules ain't from Kansas City, man, she's from Chicago… down and dirty, man, the West End. Chi-ca-go. Who told you she was from K.C.?"

"She did."

"What I just tell you? Aren't you fucking listening? You can't believe *anything* she says, she's a fucking *liar!*" Peter took one last hit and then crushed out the marijuana roach in the ashtray. He didn't even bother to hold in the smoke. "She's gonna bring you down, baby. She's gonna bring you down. She's gonna bring you down so fucking low you'll have to look up to reach the curb."

10

It was actually Stephanie who knew Jules better than anyone and who relayed to her brother, Bill, what she knew about Jules's sordid past.

Jules's real name was Joanne Luchenski. She had claimed residence, forged her birth certificate and social security card in Las Vegas, and quickly possessed a Nevada driver's license with her new alias, Julina Lukens. She was raised in Milwaukee, Wisconsin, but spent much of her adult life prostituting in Chicago. Apparently the rumor was true about her having an affair with a Chicago Police Department undercover officer, blackmailing him and forging his wife's signature on a check in order to withdraw seventy-five hundred dollars from Chicago Bank & Trust. She had even gone so far as to have arranged the forging of a fictitious State of Illinois photo driver's license claiming her to be Mrs. Thomas Bretlin, the undercover agent's wife.

Jules grew up in Walkers Point, a working class section of Milwaukee, populated mostly with German and Polish people. Hispanics and Asians dwelled on the South Side. Blacks lived on the North Side and Central Downtown Milwaukee.

When Jules was three, her father was killed on a construction site. He was part of a four-man team maneuvering an I-beam on the eighth floor of a new office building being built in Green Bay. A soaking-wet temporary plywood floor he and his fellow crew members had been walking on collapsed. Two lived, and two plunged to their deaths, including Bob Luchenski who landed on the seventh floor, his chest impaled by a six-foot high iron rod.

Jules's mother, Rita, retreated into alcoholism and lived on welfare and in a Section Eight government subsidized housing project for the next four years. She eventually sobered up enough to get a job cleaning offices in downtown buildings.

Bill hadn't quite gotten all the details straight about her mom spending three years at some kind of correctional institute for women because she tried to kill a live-in boyfriend years later. A fight ensued having something to do with Jules. The story was sketchy. "Something happened when she turned thirteen," Bill informed me in his living room while we were waiting for Jules to come back from *arranging the delivery of a few stereo systems, thank you very much.* "By that time she was already drinking and smoking pot. On her thirteenth birthday her mom's boyfriend got Jules drunk… and while mom was at work, he raped her." Bill leaned back in his duct-taped chair and lit a Marlboro. "So Jules is having sex with her mom's boyfriend but now it's in exchange for money. Dig this, she gets pregnant by the boyfriend who ends up paying for her secret abortion, only it's not a secret because her mom finds out. That's when the fight starts in the kitchen and she stabs the guy three times. Did time for attempted murder somewhere in Fond du Lac, fuck you, Wisconsin."

"What happened to Jules?"

"Ended up at some department of children and families youth shelter or some shit-place like that."

"Poor Jules…" I drifted off.

"Oh, yeah, wait, the story gets better. She has an uncle who gets appointed to act as her guardian, who turns out to be more of a scumbag than her mom's boyfriend," Bill blurts out.

"Jesus," I said to myself, beginning to have an inkling of what a tormented life Jules had led.

"The uncle is feeding drugs to Jules to set her girlfriends up with him for sex."

"She pimps her girlfriends out to her uncle?"

"You got it." Bill changed the subject, "And that 'appendix scar'? It ain't no appendix scar. It's from a knife wound… happened to her when she was sixteen… got stabbed over some boy. She was pulling gang trains at the time, a real slut."

I formed the image in my mind of Jules at sixteen letting gang members from most important (the engine) to least important (caboose) fuck her one after the other. Then I thought about the Metro North Railroad for some reason.

"I think that's when Jules got her second abortion," Bill further offered.

"What happened to her mother?" I asked.

"No idea."

"Does Jules ever talk to her?"

"I've never seen Jules talk to her mother; but I don't talk to my mother either."

"Sorry to hear that."

"That's okay, my parents have been divorced for a long time. I basically lost touch with both of them."

I sat and watched a bluebottle fly crawl up the wall. I nodded my head, indicating I knew where Bill was coming from. The truth of the matter was, I had no idea where Bill or Jules was coming from. All I did know was that Jules, Bill, Stephanie, K Dog, and people like them had worse-off lives than I did growing up. I centered on this for a second, then I thought of Jules and where she might be now; I thought of the stolen goods operation they conducted out of their house; the drugs and prostitution; the strangers that were continually coming and going; and the ethereal permanence of doom seeming to always be descending down upon us.

❀   ❀   ❀

K Dog, who was once called K-1, then K-2, K-3 up to K-6, had been just called K Dog lately. The "K" meant "Killed." The number meant how many. He decided to forgo the number system. He walked in the door first, followed by Jules laughing over a private joke of theirs on the way in. It was always better to see Jules in a good mood rather than seeing her pissed off at something stupid. Not only were they successful in unloading the Technics and Pioneer sound systems, but K Dog scored an ounce of powdered cocaine on the way home. I didn't ask, but guessed they paid about eight hundred dollars for the "z". That means after cutting it and adding lidocaine, K Dog stood to profit close to a thousand dollars—and that's without doing any of it himself or without fronting the stuff. Or if he sold by the gram, he could stand to profit almost twenty-five hundred. Better to sell by the gram rather than by a larger quantity, because each time you sell at a larger quantity, you need to drop the price a bit. Nonetheless, that's okay too because you unload the stuff faster. K Dog was able to sell three ounces in twelve hours. Of course the less a dealer keeps for himself the more profit he'll make. K Dog had the self-control to do that. Maybe that's why he was driving a Beamer.

K Dog walked into the kitchen, found two clean dinner plates, sat at the kitchen table, picked up a Bicycle playing card (the King of Diamonds) and portioned out two equally-eyeballed half-ounces for himself and Jules. At the same time, Jules went into the connecting garage, returned with a gram/ounce scale, placed it in the middle of the table, and sat down across from K Dog. He pushed one of the plates over to Jules. She slid it gently towards her, and with the Queen of Diamonds, doled out the contents of the plate onto the scale. She studied the weight.

"I need another g," Jules said. Without saying a word K Dog shoveled a corner of the playing card into his white pile and gently placed what he thought a gram should look like on top of Jules's scale as if the white powder were gold. Jules studied the weight. "Perfect."

I sat down at the table, my back against the wall, between K Dog and Jules, and lit a Marlboro. Bill sat across from me. He already had a cigarette going. We watched K Dog and Jules go through the process of adding "cut" to their product by adding a little lidocaine to the mix—a common adulterant like baby laxative. First, they each kept three and a half grams—an eight ball—for themselves, and then weighed, separated, and began to separate the remaining white powder into grams.

Rule of the street: when you're in the presence of someone who has loads of cocaine and you don't, you don't *ask* for a hit. I think it was Ralph Waldo Emerson who once wrote, "The highest price you can pay for something is to ask for it." More respect is shown to those with restraint.

K Dog shoveled the corner of the King into the white pile again. He then placed the corner directly under my left nostril. I inhaled a quick hit causing me to push my head back slightly.

"Thanks," I said not only for the hit, but for the mutual respect. "I got forty dollars."

K Dog said, "It's cool." He didn't want any money. He offered the same to Bill.

"Hey, Mickey, you want to make some money?" Jules asked me.

"Doing what?"

"Help us get rid of this stuff at the bar."

"I'd be stepping on Bones's bones."

K Dog eyed Jules like he knew I would have said that, like he and Jules had talked about this on the way home.

"He doesn't need to know," Jules said.

"Of course he's going to know. He's going to find out. You know better than that."

"That his turf?" K Dog asked.

"That's his 'hood," I answered.

K Dog looked at me on the word "hood" and nodded.

"What's he going to do?" Jules said.

"I really don't want to know," I said.

"He that tough?" K Dog asked.

"Yeah, he is, and he's got connections, too," I said. "Been to jail so many times, I don't need to personally know who those connections might be. I like my face the way it is."

"I been to jail, too. Got plenty o' connections," K Dog boasted.

"Then you know what I'm talking about," I said. I stopped him. I stopped K Dog right there.

"It's cool. We just thought we'd cut you in on the action," K Dog said.

I thought about it. There was silence. K Dog continued to gram the coke while Jules now concentrated on filling the Peruvian mountains into individualized tiny clear plastic bags. Bill sat and smoked his cigarette, mesmerized by all the white powder in front of him.

"Why me?" I asked, "Why do you want me in the action?"

"Because *you* got connections, too," K Dog said.

Again, silence. I thought about it more.

Bill said to Jules, "We got our second eviction notice today."

"And? So?"

"And, so, why don't we just pay the rent? I need your half."

"Don't worry about it," Jules said, "you'll get your money."

They let the rent slide. Jules and Bill let the water bill, the electric bill, and the phone bill slide. They let everything go even though they had the money coming in. Jules just didn't want to pay overhead.

❁   ❁   ❁

Jules liked to shoplift on Saturdays only. Her reasoning was that the stores were more crowded and therefore there were more distractions for her not to be noticed.

"I like taking small things," she volunteered as we were roaming the aisles at Robinson's in Sherman Oaks.

Her adeptness at lifting women's fragrances was as natural as a gazelle gracefully sprinting through the aisles of unfamiliar territory always on the lookout for predators. I watched as Jules swiped Elizabeth Taylor's *Passion* perfume from a display pyramid atop a cosmetic counter and quickly place it in her large exclusively-for-this-purpose Perry Ellis handbag. Next off the shelves came Ralph Lauren's *Safari*, Clinique skin care products, and *Poison* by Christian Dior.

She had the proclivity for stealing such things.

111

I tried my hand at swiping a four-ounce bottle of Ralph Lauren's *Polo* cologne from the men's department. It was easy.

❀   ❀   ❀

A *Los Angeles Times* poll found that sixty-seven percent of L.A. residents believe that another outbreak of rioting is possible within the next few years... ...prosecutors are seeking a retrial of Officer Laurence Powell in the beating of Rodney King... ...preliminary hearings began in the two-thousand-plus riot-related felony cases... ...former L.A. Raider football player Lyle Alzado, forty-three, died of inoperable brain cancer... ...a Boyle Heights woman, Anna Lizarraga, who spent the past twenty years counseling youths to stay out of gangs, was gunned down execution-style in her driveway.

11

KDog was a Crip from the Eight-Trays set. The Eight-Trays were a deep set with a membership of over three hundred gangsters. Their territory covered a lot of ground on the east side of the Harbor Freeway: 67th Street to Century Boulevard, Vermont to Western Avenues and from 18th to 83rd Streets from Vermont to Van Ness Boulevard. Florence and Normandie, where the riots first began, are located in Crip territory.

At the age of eleven, Kendel Williams was initiated into the Crips. Initiation in Crip parlance is known as a "conscription." Four of his soon-to-be fellow gang members pommeled Kendel until he bled and couldn't get up. But Kendel had to rise to the occasion of his next conscription, which was to steal a car. It was a '65 Mustang.

"Sixty-five Mustangs is easy. All you have to do is take a metal clothes hanger and touch the alternator and battery at the same time," K Dog instructed me, "then you jus' get in an' drive."

"What about '91 Mustangs?" I asked, referring obviously to mine.

K Dog formed his right hand into an imaginary gun pointing his forefinger and thumb extended at my head. "Ya jus' aks."

Kendel Williams received his gang moniker quickly. The day after his initiation he killed his first enemy Blood on 66th Street three blocks from where Kendel, his mama, and two younger sisters lived. Bloods were doing a drive-by in a Chevy Nova upon Kendel's circle of homeboys when Kendel, anticipating what was going down, retaliated by quickly pulling out a blue steel .44 Bulldog revolver from the rear waistband of his baggy khakis and popped the driver in the head with two bullets. The Nova jumped the curb, missed hitting a small boy on a bicycle, and hit a tree; the set of Crips ran from the scene. Bloods stumbled out of the demolition and ran in the opposite direction. Everyone disappeared except the dead sixteen-year-old Blood slumped over the steering wheel. No one got caught. Kendel immediately became a Killer. K-1. There were going to be other shootings.

Crips kill more Bloods than Bloods kill Crips. Crips kill more Crips than Bloods kill Crips. According to an FBI report, "...one out of every four Crips is in jail for murder, or has done time for murder... three out of four Crips have been arrested for weapons-related charges..."

K-2—as he was known by the ninth grade—walked out of Horace Mann Junior High School on 71st Street after being suspended for fighting. He never returned. At that time he was making over one thousand dollars per day selling crack. He used the money to purchase guns, clothes, jewelry, CDs, more drugs, and to gain power in the 'hood with better connections. Eventually, he worked his way up unloading twenty-five hundred dollars worth of crack, heroin, and marijuana per day. Then he got busted. That cost him eight months at Los Padinos Juvenile Hall in nearby Downey.

Juvenile Hall instigated K-2's attitude to become more militant and savvy. He now was initiated into the halls of juvenile detention. This made him angry. It made him proud. Eager. While in Juvenile Hall he didn't just learn his required schooling, but he amassed a knowledge that would do him the real service he needed to know "on the outs." He learned from other incarcerated peers how to "put in work": how to rob, burglarize, car jack, how to fight, how to survive.

After his release he took this knowledge with him to the streets and to his fellow gang members who had already "overstood" the meaning of their lives or understood what was to become. Juvenile Hall was K-2's training wheels that reeled bad things in motion. It was the worst place he could have ever gone to. It taught him nothing about recovery. He came out a fifteen-year-old gangsta more ready to commit crime and to kill.

By the time K-2 turned eighteen and was called K-4, he had been stabbed in thirteen different places, shot twice, in and out of Martin Luther King Hospital a total of six times, amassed a body count of four dead Bloods—never convicted—sentenced to a total of thirteen months at Camp Kilpatrick (the next step after Juvenile Hall) for "assaulting an officer" (California Penal code 243), and another nine months in Youth Hall for Grand Theft Auto. He had spent half as much of his time as a Crip incarcerated as he did on the streets. His mama cried herself to sleep every night.

"Jus' protectin' my family," was Kendel's reasoning and logic.

In 1989, K-4 was convicted of a murder he never committed. Irony stole his body and sent it to Soledad State Prison. His soul was already destined to be there. After two years the true murderer in the case, another Crip, was apprehended, arrested, and convicted. K-4 was released.

Only recently did K Dog venture into the San Fernando Valley to steal cars. He and his homeboys specialized in stealing BMWs, Mercedes, Saabs, Audis, Porsches, and other high-priced automobiles. During this time period K Dog was at the Wayfarer Motel fucking a white girl named Stephanie. Stephanie introduced K Dog to Jules. Jules had an "organized" connection that also specialized in the theft of high-priced autos. She introduced him to Louie.

❀   ❀   ❀

Every time K Dog, Jules, and Bill were to pull off a GTA, they'd use another stolen car to do it. That night it was a 1990 Ford Taurus. Bill was driving. Jules was sitting in the front passenger seat. K Dog and I were sitting in the back. I was behind Jules. K Dog was behind Bill. We were on our way to Encino. We all wore gloves and were dressed in black.

Their modus operandi varied. Sometimes they'd just pull up to a parked car in a Sav-On or Von's or Ralph's food market parking lot and "jimmie" the car door between the rubber trim and window with a device made of spring steel, a rubber handle on one end, and a series of notches on the other end to unlock the locking mechanism. Cars with digital numbered door locks were disengaged by disconnecting the battery first.

Sometimes K Dog and Bill did the "bump and take." Bill, who would be driving, bumped gently into the rear of a vehicle with a lone driver at a stop sign in a remote residential neighborhood. When the irritated driver would get out to inspect the damage, Bill would get out too, and talk his way over to the victim's driver door; Bill would then jump into the victim's driver seat and speed off. At the same time, K Dog would slide over, take the steering wheel of the car they were driving in, speed off, and meet Bill at a predetermined spot where the original car that was also stolen was abandoned. They used this method to upgrade.

This particular night the plan was a little more complex, a scheme K Dog, Jules, and Bill hadn't yet tried. I assumed they varied their methods. They needed a fourth person to pull this one off.

Guilty by association: that was me.

"Never do the same thing too many times," Jules advised. "Always do something different so the five-o don't see a pattern."

I nodded my head in agreement.

No drugs were carried on these excursions—not that they weren't consumed beforehand. In fact, a couple of beers and a few lines of coke gave us just the right edge of confidence we needed.

"We're doing two cars tonight," Jules said matter-of-factly.

"Two cars," I echoed.

"At the same time," Jules stated. K Dog and I looked at each other, me with doubt, him with certainty.

"We be mountin' up," K Dog said. "We on a mission. There be no slippin'."

I nodded my head again in agreement and then looked down at the Browning 9-millimeter automatic K Dog had tucked in the front

DANGEROUS LOVE

waistband of his baggy black khakis. I looked up at his profile; his dark brown eyes stared straight ahead. I turned my head and did the same.

Bill was obeying the speed limit driving west on Ventura Boulevard. Our destination was Alutia, an exotic Mediterranean restaurant. Alutia was just upscale enough where an upper-class clientele dined but no valet parking was provided. Besides street parking, additional parking was available at the rear of the restaurant where it happened to have been a little darker than the usual parking lot at the rear of a swank restaurant. Also, Los Angeles, and especially the Valley, has alleyways where delivery trucks and cars could drive behind stores and restaurants that run parallel to the main streets, avenues, and boulevards.

It was Bill's job to scout and find these ideal locations for their GTA missions and to plan the getaway routes.

Bill took a left on Balboa Boulevard and another left into the alley. It was about nine-thirty p.m. He pulled alongside a row of bougainvilleas within sight of the rear entrance of the restaurant, a rear kitchen door, and the alley. LAPD often patrol these alleys, so it was particularly important that we could see the entire area from where we sat. The plan was for Bill and Jules to be lookouts while K Dog would jimmie a car door open. He'd then quickly disconnect the alarm if there was one, and I would jump into this first car and take off. K Dog would then jimmie the second car and take off in that one. If there was anything out of the ordinary or if anyone arrived on the scene, Bill would slightly toot the horn once, quickly, to indicate to K Dog and me that someone was approaching. It could have been anything from a car pulling into the parking lot, to a woman walking a dog, to an LAPD Crown Victoria cruising the alley. It meant for us to stop what we were doing, look around, hide, let the danger pass, or get out of there. Bill and Jules opening the car doors and stepping out of the car pretending to be going into the restaurant meant for us to abort the mission and to split up.

"Yo, bitch, gimme a cigarette," K Dog said to Jules.

Jules handed K Dog a Newport.

"Don't light the cigarette," came from Bill.

K Dog lit the cigarette. "Why?"

"Because it'll attract attention."

"Shiiit, nobody here."

"I said put the fucking cigarette out!"

K Dog took a deep drag from the Newport and blew the smoke slowly into the rear of Bill's head. K Dog then took another drag, looked at me and smiled defiantly. He was in a bad mood that night.

"Yo, no one orders K Dog what he can or cannot do."

"We're not ordering you," Jules said calmly, "just be cool."

K Dog went into rap mode: "Hey, I ain't no fool, I be cool, you know that Jule, I'm bulletproof, got a gat by my side, walk with stride, got lots of pride, I'm bulletproof, that's me, no Rodney King, just a thing, I'm bulletproof, yeah, bulletproof, and I be hangin', bangin', slangin', that's me—"

"Shut the fuck up," Bill said.

"Say what, you mothafucka? You need K Dog for this action."

"Both of you shut the fuck up," Jules said. "Let's get this over with."

Bill and Jules got out of the car while K Dog and I hunched down in the back seat. (Previously, we'd disconnected the interior light.) After Bill and Jules closed the doors K Dog and I sat up. We watched Bill and Jules slowly walk towards the rear entrance of the restaurant. They purposefully walked slow, pretending to be talking, and at the same time searching into each of the parked cars to make sure no one was inside either talking or kissing or whatever. They scouted the lot to determine which two cars we were going to break into and if the whole set-up, strategy, location, and *feeling* was right and feasible to go through with. Once all these factors were in place and no one was around Bill and Jules made their way back to the car.

"There's a black Infiniti Q forty-five parked between a gray Volvo and a white Saab half-way down on the right. Three cars down, diagonally across the lot is a white Lexus SC four hundred parked between a red convertible Audi and a black Thunderbird," Bill told K Dog and me after he and Jules returned to the car.

K Dog and I went to work.

Bill and Jules pulled in first at our drop-off location inside South Bay Auto Repair in Culver City. K Dog was behind me as we drove into the large six-car garage. A short Italian-looking mechanic with beady eyes, dressed in grease-drenched overalls, pushed a large red button on the wall causing heavy metal doors behind us to close. We were safe. No sirens in the distance were getting closer. No flashing red, white and blue lights of the LAPD. A successful mission.

We wasted no time.

"You have the money?" Jules asked the mechanic.

"No, I don't got the money. I'm supposed to have the money, but I don't; you gotta talk to Louie," the mechanic said.

"What you mean you don't got the money? C.O.D. mothafucker," K Dog said approaching the mechanic. "You think we be stuck on stupid?"

The mechanic looked at K Dog with distaste. "I said I don't have it. I don't know what happened. It was supposed to be delivered, but I don't have it. I don't know—"

"We're supposed to get four-thousand dollars for each car," Bill explained.

The mechanic shrugged his shoulders and raised his hands and arms in the air. Jules took the lead. "Let me get this straight. You said the money is supposed to be *delivered?* But you don't have it yet?"

"That's right."

"Who's delivering the money?"

"I don't know. One of Louie's men."

We all stood there in tableaux and looked at each other. Four thousand for each car would have been two thousand each for Bill, Jules, K Dog, and myself. Two grand for one hour of work. But there was no money.

K Dog was not happy. "What you mean you don't know. You don't know? I'll smoke you, you say that one mo' time."

The mechanic said again, defiantly, "I said, I don't know. I don't know what else to tell you." Pause. "You gotta talk to Louie."

"I ain't gotta talk to no one but *you*. Now, one mo' time, you holding out on us? Are you lyin'?"

The mechanic challenged K Dog. "Fuck you, I ain't lying."

K Dog took another step towards the mechanic, now only inches away. "You got eight thousand for us or not, mothafucker?" K Dog asked.

"I said NO. How many times do I have to tell you?"

"He said he doesn't know," Bill interjected.

"He don't know," K Dog continued staring at the mechanic, "You mad doggin' me?"

"What?" the mechanic asked annoyed.

"Who else here?" K Dog asked, staring into the mechanic's eyes with hate.

"Me only."

K Dog pulled out his Browning and shot the mechanic in the face. Blood and brains exploded out the back of his head as he jerked backwards and fell to the cement floor. More blood and brains spilled out from beneath his head.

Bill, Jules, and I jumped back astonished. My ears were ringing. The odor of cordite filled the garage.

"You fucking asshole!" Jules screamed at K Dog.

"I ain't in a no good mood," K Dog said calmly as he put another bullet into the dead man's chest. "Chalk another one-eighty-seven up for the K. Kill or be killed."

"We gotta get outta here," Bill said.

"We have to take the cars with us," I said, holding back vomit as I stared down at the dead mechanic.

"Where we gonna take 'em?" Bill countered.

K Dog strode across the garage and into an office area.

"Where *you* going?" Jules yelled to him.

"Looking for money."

"Forget the fucking money. He was telling us the truth."

"Here," K Dog said as he rang open a cash register. "There be some money in here."

We were all still wearing gloves so there was no possibility of fingerprints.

"Hurry up," Bill said, then, "What are we going to do with the cars?"

"Leave the fucking cars, we be outta here," K Dog shouted from the office.

"We can't, with this dead guy here; the cops will trace it all back to Louie," Jules said.

The three of us thought for a moment. K Dog was grabbing green bills out of the register's drawer.

"L-A-X," I said.

"Let's go," Bill agreed.

K Dog and I followed Bill and Jules to Los Angeles Airport. We parked the cars near Bradley International Terminal and then jumped into the Taurus.

We drove north on the San Diego Freeway to the house in confused silence.

K Dog split the money from the cash register. Ninety-two dollars each. Hostile words between Jules, Bill, and K Dog were spoken, but mostly a lot of thinking was going on. We were responsible for killing someone connected to the Mob.

12

Jules arrived to the conclusion that she had to make up a story to tell Louie. That the mechanic was already dead when we got to South Bay Auto Repair. We saw that the register was open and empty, indicating a robbery. Would Louie buy it? Probably not, but we had no choice. Jules figured it was better for us to get in contact with Louie first instead of him getting in contact with us. We were nervous, except for K Dog. He was accustomed to this sort of thing—killing.

Jules called Louie at his home in Vegas. He lived in an upper-class neighborhood facing the Las Vegas Country Club. We heard Jules's side of the conversation.

"Is Louie there?

"It's Jules.

"Jules, he knows me.

"Yeah, that one.

"Do you know where he is? I need to get in touch with him right away. It's an emergency.

"I'd rather tell *him*." Jules was getting annoyed. She cupped her hand over the telephone's mouthpiece and said, "Fucking bitch."

"Do you have his number there? I don't have it.

"You can give it to *me*," and then, "Fuck." Jules slammed the handset down. "She hung up on me."

"Who hung up on you?" Bill asked.

"Some fucking cunt bitch. All she said was he's in Laughlin."

"We have to go to Laughlin," I said.

"You think that's a good idea?" Bill said.

"Mickey's right. I don't know what else to do. We can't just sit here. You," Jules glared at K Dog, "better find yourself a hiding place."

"Dis nigga don't hide," K Dog said.

"Do you know where he stays in Laughlin?" I asked.

Jules dropped her glare from K Dog and paced. "He keeps a suite at one of the casinos, I forgot which," she finally answered. "Laughlin's not that big, it's not like Vegas; we shouldn't have a hard time finding him."

❁　❁　❁

Laughlin was becoming the new gambling mecca of the Southwest, located ninety miles south of Las Vegas at the very corner tip of Nevada, bordering California and Arizona at the northeast edge of the Mojave Desert on the banks of the Colorado River. The area was once known as South Pointe, due to the fact that it was the most southerly part of Clark County and Nevada. The construction of Davis Dam, completed in 1953, brought workers to the area. In 1966, Southern California Edison purchased thousands of acres of land to build a coal-fed powerplant. More people. That same year, a developer named Don Laughlin opened Riverside Resort and later the Bobcat Club, which evolved into the Nevada Club and then the Golden Nugget. Other casinos opened, and in 1968, the U.S. postal inspector officially named the area Laughlin. Gambling flourished and a new center for the gaming industry was born. More casinos were eventually built, including Harrah's in 1988 and the Flamingo Hotel in 1990.

Louie had something to do with Harrah's and the Flamingo but I didn't know what at the time Jules and I were heading east, top down, on Interstate 40, through the San Bernardino Mountains, at three a.m., Wednesday morning. Travel time from Los Angeles to

Laughlin is about four hours and almost three hundred miles of driving. I had to be at work at six that night. Jules assured me that "this won't take long" and that our lives were in danger if we didn't straighten this out and that I wouldn't have a job to go back to if I was dead from one of Louie's fat fucking flunkies.

A person does a lot of thinking while driving through the Mojave Desert at ninety miles per hour while the sun is coming up over Missouri. We were passing through the practically nonexistent-town-in-the-middle-of-nowhere Ludlow, and listening to "Oh God, I Wish I Was Home Tonight," by Rod Stewart, blasting through the car's radio speakers when the question occurred to me of where was I going to pull over and how was I going to snuff Jules and bury her body in the night desert for casting me in this B- picture?

Living in cities all my life, I'd never experienced the wide open spaces of a desert, or such a black sky with its billion pinpoints of starry lights—combined with the hot dry air and effects from the samples of drugs I was taking. Before we left the San Fernando Valley, we made sure we had plenty of methamphetamines, including six white crosses, one gram of crank, and one eight ball of powdered cocaine.

"How do you know Louie?" I asked Jules in a false feeling of soberness.

"We go back a long way," Jules answered after lighting a Newport. Jules thought about it and then studied me. "Ten years. …helped me out while I lived in Chicago for a while."

"Chicago?"

"He was one of my first clients when I was escorting. He'd take me to places, nice places on the West Side, have dinners, watch out for me. He'd turn me on to his friends. They all had money. Lots of money. They were all connected. They treated me good. Especially Louie. He knew I was going through times with my mom and all."

"What about your mom?"

Jules looked at me; her past was nothing but outtakes on an editing room floor.

"You don't have to tell me," I told her.

"My dad died when I was three. My mom went downhill after that, booze, drugs, unemployed. All kinds of men would stay over, live with us for a while, fight with my mom and leave. One guy who was living with us raped me on my thirteenth birthday. I didn't tell anybody. I was too scared of what he might do. Then he started to force himself on me other times. I told him I was going to tell my mom. But he gave me money to let him fuck me and to shut up about it. Fucking creep. I got pregnant and had to have an abortion. He paid for it, but eventually my mom found out. She stabbed him with a kitchen knife. She ended up in prison for attempted murder. I got shuffled around between social service agencies and foster homes and finally ended up living with an uncle—another fucking creep. Anyway, after my mom got out of the hole the state wouldn't let me live with her because they considered her an unfit mother. I ran away from my uncle's, quit school, and started sleeping around. That's when I started walking the streets making money, selling myself to any guy who had cash for a blow job or fuck."

"How old were you?"

"I just turned seventeen."

"Were you still in school?"

"School wasn't even a reality for me. By that time I had been way into drugs and fucking off anyway. Then I started hating everybody – boys, men, girls who were supposed to be my friends. I hated my mom. I thought my mom hated me. I had no one. But I knew I was attractive. I put that to use. I cleaned up real good and took the bus to Chicago on Fridays. By Sunday, I'd make over a grand. But I didn't blow the money. I saved it. I opened an account at a Chicago bank and actually saved the money. I stopped using drugs to make myself look better and then got myself a small apartment on the West Side. That's when I met Louie. He took care of me, paid for the apartment, and made me feel better about myself. I told him my mom wasn't doin' so good, she was sick and even though I hated her I still loved her. I know that doesn't make any sense…"

"Yeah, it does," I said, consoling her.

"Anyway, Louie helped my mom. She didn't have health insurance or anything, she was working cleaning offices, and then she got sick. She ended up getting cancer, bone marrow cancer. Louie paid for her hospital bills. In eighty-four she... died."

I looked at Jules; tears were dripping down her cheeks. She wiped them away, sniffled, turned away, put her head back on the seat, and looked up into the blackness of the sky.

"After my mom died there was no reason to go back to Milwaukee."

"So you're not from Kansas City?"

She looked half-way in my direction, the hint of a coy smile, "I was born there, that's all," she said.

We took the River Road exit and made our way onto Needles Highway before continuing northeast for about ten miles to Laughlin. The sun was rising over Bullhead City across the Colorado River in Arizona. Bullhead City was named for Bull's Head Rock, a geological formation on the Colorado River. This natural landmark was once used as a navigation point by steamboat captains. Now the rock is submerged beneath Lake Mojave, a reservoir five hundred fifty square miles of water, cliffs, sandy beaches, and more rock.

"Find Casino Drive, that's the main strip," Jules said, "then pull over at the first place we see to eat and let's have breakfast."

"You're hungry?" I asked, not believing the amphetamines we had been ingesting did not curb her appetite.

"Yeah, I'm way the fuck hungry."

We ate in a coffee shop at the Riverside Resort. Jules had three scrambled eggs, a double order of bacon, extra home-fries, four slices of burnt rye toast, one large glass of orange juice, two large glasses of milk, three glasses of water, and four cups of coffee. I had six half-filled cups of coffee. The bill came to four dollars, seventy-eight cents. I watched Jules gulp down her food while I read the headlines of the *Vegas Sun*. Las Vegas rocked with riots. Because of Rodney King and the L.A. Riots, racial riots were beginning to rise up in other cities across the nation.

❁   ❁   ❁

The cow-eyed girl behind the registration desk at the Riverside Resort said there was no one by the name of Louie Vicente staying at the hotel.

We got the same response from each of the hotels along the strip: the Regency, the Edgewater, the Colorado Belle, the Pioneer, the Ramada Express, and the Nugget. The clerks behind the registration desks at the Flamingo and Harrah's both said, "Sorry, but we can't divulge that information."

We kept on moving, retracing our steps, going back to the same casinos, walking on the floors, through bars, lounges, and restaurants. I traded in a ten dollar bill for a roll of quarters and played the slots. I lost.

I thought I saw Louie a few times. Jules told me it wasn't him. Jules then remembered that he liked to play golf, so we drove over to the Emerald River Golf Course two miles south of Harrah's. Jules inquired at the sports shop, but no Louie Vicente was playing golf that day and they wouldn't tell us where we could find him either. We went back to Harrah's.

We stood in the middle of the casino and both noticed at the same time what must have been a newlywed couple, their arms entwined behind each other's lower backs, stars in their eyes, soft breaths of love from their lips.

"Let's get married," Jules said to me. I said, "No thanks, but thanks for asking." We joked about getting married and then let it go. A few moments later I looked at Jules and thought what it would be like to be married to her. Were marriage and a normal life something Jules had always secretly wanted? Would a fairytale fairyland life of happiness and bliss change Alice in Wonderland's ways? Was long lasting love something she felt she could never have? Was this her cause for resentment? How would her life have been different if her father hadn't died when he did? If her mother hadn't turned out to be a depressant drug-induced alcoholic? If things hadn't gone awry?

Harrah's had their own private sandy beach along the river. Jules and I sat in lounge chairs, drank Bloody Marys, and watched the activity of adults sunning themselves, strolling along the beach, and wading in the river.

I went to find a pay phone and called work. Karen answered the phone. I lied to her saying I was in Las Vegas and that my car was "missing" and that I think it was towed away because it was parked illegally and that I was calling around and walking around trying to find it and if she would call one of the other bartenders to work for me that would be just peachy. Karen said she'd work the double and was glad to do it because she needed the extra money anyway because she was saving for a new car herself and she knew what a pain in the ass it was to have a car sometimes but hey you need one. Karen went on and on about damn cars when a click in the phone interrupted us and a woman's mechanical voice came on the line saying I needed to add more money… Karen came back on the line and I said hurriedly that I'd definitely see her tomorrow but at the same time asking myself if tomorrow will ever come if we find Louie and he ends up smoking Jules and me—both of us getting buried in the desert.

When I exited the rear of the hotel to return to the beach I saw a guy sitting in my lounge chair talking to Jules. I stopped, took a step to the side, stood and watched. I then saw them both get up and enter another entrance into the hotel. I figured Jules had connected with someone who knew Louie. I was wrong, because twenty-five minutes later she came back to sit down and told me she just made a hundred bucks giving some guy a blow job in his room.

"We're gonna need money if we can't find Louie today and have to stay until tomorrow," Jules rationalized.

"Look," I said, "if we don't find Louie by tonight, I'm outta here."

"You think we're gonna find him in one day?"

We didn't find Louie. He found us.

The sun was going down across the river over the mountain range of Arizona. I turned and looked at Jules. She was asleep—or passed out. Even though we had been doing amphetamines since we left L.A., we were both exhausted. No matter how much speed one does you're going to have to come down sooner or later. Just like everything else, what goes up must come down. And Bloody Marys are a great settler of putting you back in your place from uppers and making you crash.

In the drone of a mindless sleep I felt a nudging at my feet. When I opened my eyes, standing before me were two casually dressed men both in tan chino slacks, one was wearing a black Izod shirt and brown leather sandals with black socks; the other was wearing a red cowboy shirt, cowboy boots, and cowboy hat. A call from Central Casting. Both were silhouetted against the glow of a distant sun disappearing, its radiance now crimsoned in a clear desert sky.

One of the men said, "We hear you're looking for Mister Louie Vicente."

13

The name of the houseboat was *The Saint*. Louie's moniker was "The Saint", as in Louie The Saint Vicente. Louie was called The Saint because he had a special affinity towards Saint Michael. And Louie named his houseboat, which was really a seventy-two-foot custom-built fresh water yacht, *The Saint* in honor of St. Michael because St. Michael was a very special saint. Louie believed that St. Michael was a "bad motherfucker," and that if you knew anything about anything you would respect St. Michael—and Louie. Louie prayed to St. Michael every Sunday when he tried to make church. He prayed to St. Michael for protection on the job and to assist Louie in tracking down his client's customers who maybe "forgot to pay" their markers. However, out of the last month of Sundays, Louie missed church once and that was because he had to level the praying, ah, playing field. A man from Rock Springs, Wyoming, had run out on his marker from a famous casino, necessitating Louie and "Fingers" to go find the man and teach him that running out on an IOU from a famous casino without paying the debt he owed was like stealing and stealing wasn't Christian-like, never mind that the man from Rock Springs was a Jew named Rosenguard. So, Louie had the Jew sign over his car, a 1992 BMW, to Louie for one dollar so Louie could drive the Beamer back to Nevada on Monday and resell it for more than what the man owed the casino, which was about eight thousand dollars. Fingers crushed a few of the man's appendages just to drive the lesson home further that the man should not steal.

The two men who brought Jules and me to see Louie on *The Saint* also had monikers; one was the aforementioned Fingers, as in Tommy Fingers Bonatto; the other was "Pumpkin Head" as in Tommy Pumpkin Head Zaroti. Yes, both were named Tommy, so the nicknames came in handy. The cowboy was Pumpkin Head.

Jules and I were patted-down and searched by Fingers and Pumpkin Head. They reached into our pockets, pulled out our cocaine and tossed it into Lake Mojave. I heard Louie's voice inside my head from when I first met him at Jules's house: *no drugs, I don't want any drugs in this house.* It was a good thing we weren't holding much and that we still had stash hidden in a magnetic Hide-a-Key underneath the Mustang attached to the rear of the gasoline tank.

The houseboat, *The Saint*, was floating pretty with its glow of house lights at Katherine Landing, Arizona, eight miles from Laughlin, across the Colorado River on Lake Mojave. Burning talons of deep reds and oranges spread across a slow-fading sky. Dusk was descending as I was wondering if I would ever see another sunset, not only one as beautiful as this one, but any sunset at all. Or would I, at the very least, have my fingers intact?

The interior of the boat looked like an opulent penthouse suite atop a famous casino. Louie must have liked luxurious living on the water. Teakwood walls and cabinets, glass and chromium tables, expensive tan leather sofas, love seats and chairs gave the salon a homey feeling. R.C. Gorman Southwestern lithographs of Navajo Indians were displayed on the walls. A Remington sculpture of a cowboy on a raging horse was stationed on a shelf above the multi-component stereo system. Sitting on another shelf was a thirty-two-inch Sony Trinitron television and Sony videocassette recorder/player. The galley at the rear was sparkling clean as though no one had ever cooked a meal there. I knew this couldn't have been true because Louie in fact very much liked to cook. No aroma of burning brownies this time; however, I thought I detected the simmering aroma of tomato sauce. The lighting was low-key. Louie, with half-lensed reading glasses perched at the end of his nose, wearing a black terry-cloth and gold piping robe, sat comfortably in a plush tan leather upright-positioned recliner, listening to classical music. A string quartet? Vivaldi? Mozart? The man, The Saint, was also reading a book.

Pumpkin Head and Fingers escorted Jules and me into the salon and pointed for us to sit on the sofa across from Louie. We sank into the soft cushioned leather and looked around. "Nice place, Louie," was Jules's opening statement. "We never would have found you."

Louie peered over the top of his reading glasses at Jules and said, "I'm not easily found."

Fingers and Pumpkin Head turned and walked up on the rear deck. They sat themselves in lounge chairs, their backs to us but within hearing distance. I saw motion directly behind Louie in what must have been a rear bedroom beyond the galley at the end of a short hallway. A beautiful slender and tanned brunette naked woman appeared from inside the bedroom and crossed to the door; she sneaked a direct peek at Jules and me and then closed the door gently. Louie picked up a remote control lying next to him and shut off the sweet soothing sounds of violins. He then took off his glasses, placed a bookmark between two clumps of pages and placed the book down in front of us on the low glass and chromium coffee table. I stared at the upside down book until I was able to read the large printed letters: *Unto the Sons* by Gay Talese. Two other books lay on the table: *Double Deuce* by Robert B. Parker, and *Harlot's Ghost* by Norman Mailer. Louie stared at Jules then glanced at me then stared back at Jules. He held on to the remote control.

"I thought I told you *never* to come to me… that I would always come to you, if need be," Louie said directly to Jules without a more friendlier greeting and without blinking.

"I called you in Vegas, some girl answered the—"

Louie raised his right hand for Jules to stop talking. It was hard not to notice the giant gold and sapphire pinky ring he was wearing. *God, he was just like out of the movies.* "I know," he quickly said, then he turned to me, "And you're in this now." It was more of a statement than a question.

"I told you we needed a fourth," Jules said confidently.

"You should o' listened to me and stayed away from her," he exhorted, gazing at me.

I looked at Jules; she was looking at Louie and what was that, *smiling*? No, smirking.

"Maybe you're right," I said into his unblinking dark brown eyes. Jules's smirk widened. The bitch.

I was about to light a cigarette until Louie said no smoking. He studied us for a while. He nodded his head; his eyes went back and forth from Jules to me from Jules to me to Jules.

"What?" Jules said.

"You know there's a certain kind of fish they have in these waters, they're called 'cutthroat' trout. Cutthroat trout. Now ain't that a helluva name for a fish?"

"Yeah, so?" Jules said.

"Why you goin' round askin' for me? That's a stupid thing to do. Why are you *here*? Something go wrong in Culver City?"

Jules and I had talked about it on the way to Laughlin, what she was going to tell Louie... how we walked in on a dead guy... how when we got to South Bay Auto Repair we found this mechanic guy dressed in dirty overalls lying on the cement floor inside the garage and how he wasn't moving and the blood... oh, the blood... and how we didn't know what to do... and we looked around and saw that the cash register was opened or broken into and that we should get out of there fast because we had no reason to be there in the first place with *three* stolen vehicles in our possession and that we certainly didn't want any trouble or to get Louie implicated in any way in what we saw... but instead, Jules said, "K Dog killed the mechanic."

Huh?

Louie didn't blink an eye. "I see. Tell me what happened."

Jules told him exactly what happened, how the mechanic said he didn't have the money, that Louie had the money, that the money was supposed to be delivered but it wasn't, and how K Dog got pissed off at the mechanic, shot him, shot him two times, and then took what little money was in the cash register.

Louie sat there and listened and when Jules was done explaining what really did happen Louie said, "I'm glad you decided to tell me the truth for once. You just saved your life, your friend's here, and Bill's." Louie didn't say anything about K Dog's life being saved though. "And do you know how I know it is the truth?" Louie said and clicked on the Sonys. His question was answered by what we saw on the large screen.

We watched the four of us from the previous night inside the garage of South Bay Auto Repair. We watched again how K Dog had smoked the mechanic. *We were on videotape.*

Jules was impressed. She smiled a wide grin. "You fuck, Louie." I was a little shaken myself.

Jules looked at me and laughed. I didn't think it was so funny. Louie didn't think it was so funny. He said, "The tape wasn't even intentional. The garage has a security camera that's always on."

"Well, what about the money? Why wasn't the money there?" Jules asked, always getting to the point.

Louie didn't say anything. He ejected the tape, got up out of his chair, crossed to the VCR and took out the videotape. "Hey, Pumpkin Head..." Pumpkin Head stood at the doorway from the rear deck. Louie tossed him the tape. "Get rid of this." Pumpkin Head caught the tape with both hands and said, "Right, boss." He then turned. Louie then walked into the galley, picked up a large wooden spoon, lifted the lid of a large pot sitting on a burner of the stove and stirred its contents. The whiff of tomato sauce filled the air. "You kids want somethin'? Maybe a soda pop or somethin'?"

"Gin 'n' tonic?" I answered.

"No alcohol on board, mate. This is a clean and sober ship."

"What about the *money*, Louie?" Jules repeated.

"Are the cars still at LAX?" Louie asked as if by rote and then tasting the tomato sauce overspilling on the oversized spoon.

"They should be," I said, still not realizing where all this was going.

"... got the claim tickets right here," Jules said as she reached into her cut-off fringed Jordache's and produced two parking claim tickets. She threw them on the glass table in front of us.

Louie didn't even look. "Good." He put the lid back on the pot, placed the spoon down and grabbed himself an Evian Spring Water from the refrigerator. No one said anything for a while. "There was a fuck up," and then as if annoyed by himself, "a communication problem. The guy at South Bay was supposed to receive ten thousand from us, two for him, eight for youz guys. But there was a fuck up. He didn't get the money on time. What he told you he thought was the truth... gettin' it from me. He never did have it. Our guy got there too late. Fuckin' idiot."

"Maybe he should have left a little earlier," Jules added.

Louie gave her a look. He then crossed the room, opened a cigar box on a shelf near the television and reached in. He walked back to his recliner, sat down, and threw down sixteen lavender-colored gambling chips next to the parking claim tickets. "Each one's worth five hundred."

"Dollars?" Jules asked.

"Of course dollars. And make sure you cash them in because they ain't gonna do you no good in L.A.... fuckin' place."

Jules looked at me, "Maybe we'll play 'em."

"Look, do youz-selves a favor, go to a casino, cash the things in, and get the fuck outta town. You're lucky I'm even payin' youz."

"What about the dead guy?" Jules had to ask.

"Fuck the dead guy. There ain't no dead guy. He just disappeared. The wife thinks he ran out on her. We made sure she thinks he ran out on her." Louie seemed disappointed with himself about the whole matter.

"So what's next?" I asked.

Louie leaned over, picked up the LAX parking claim tickets, "I'll tell ya what's next," and tore the tickets in halves.

Jules and I traded a look.

"It's over, done, *fini*! Youz guys, me, everybody."

"What are you talking about?" I asked.

"I'm outta this business," Louie said glancing at the torn tickets. "I'm goin' straight. Gonna open a gift shop down here, callin' it 'Scavenger's Find,' souvenirs, flags, banners, ashtrays, jewelry, turquoise. Little miniature London Bridges... hey, do you know they got the real fuckin' London Bridge here? They transported the fuckin' thing brick-by-fuckin'-brick from fuckin' England and then put it back together. It's down at Lake Havasu. Ain't that somethin'? In the middle of the fuckin' desert the London Bridge. Anyway, gonna sell crap like that."

"You're gonna fence jewelry, aren't you?" Jules chimed in.

"I never said that. Did you hear me say that?"

"C'mon, Louie, who're you kiddin'?"

"Gonna take a chance on the straight life—no more gamblin' either, no more cards, craps, horses, football—nothin'! Everything I do from now on is calculated. Programmed to win. No more fuck ups."

"I don't understand. You're making no sense," Jules interjected.

"It's over, I said. And you I want outta my life," Louie continued with pointed finger, "you're too much trouble. I don't want anything to do with you no more."

"Oh yeah? Well Mickey and I were thinkin', maybe we would stay down here, you know, live down here." Jules said.

"What? Whattaya talkin'?" Louie was surprised.

"Not stay here as in *here*," looking around indicating The Boat, *The Saint*, "but in Laughlin. Mickey and I'll get a place. It ain't so bad. Kind o' nice. You can hook us up with a couple jobs. Mickey'll tend bar and I'll cocktail waitress, maybe do a little business on the side… work at your gift shop or something…"

"You're kiddin' me, right? You're jokin' on me."

"C'mon Louie, Los Angeles sucks, you know that," and then she turned to me, "Right?"

Jules's idea of staying in Laughlin was news to me. Jules laughed. She looked at me and laughed. I looked at her not knowing what she was doing. Did she have a hidden agenda she obviously hadn't told me about? We never talked about living in Laughlin.

"Look, I want you as far away from me as possible. Do you understand that? I've had enough of you," Louie said to Jules.

"That hurts me, Louie, that really hurts me."

"What am I gonna do with you? How many times do I tell you to clean up your act, get yourself together, get a respectable job—any job, do the right thing. Maybe get married, have kids, lead a normal life."

"Like you?"

"Don't get smart with me, little gal. I wish I did lead a normal life... wish somebody had given me the chance to get out when I was sportsbookin' back in Chicago."

"You haven't done bad for yourself," Jules said.

"It looks that way, don't it? Funny. I got the Nevada Gaming Control Board dickin' down my throat for attempted bribery and money launderin' in Vegas that I was actually *acquitted* with; the Organized Crime Strike Force is blowin' up my ass for that attempted murder rap in Cleveland I *beat*. Huh, they think there's organized crime in Nevada. There hasn't been organized crime in Nevada since the Gamin' Commission suspended the Stardust's license in eighty-three for skimmin', and since Lefty split the scene and they found Tony Spilotro and his brother under a corn field sixty miles southeast of Chicago. And, don't remind me that the Chicago Crime Commission is accusin' me of racketeerin'. I'm not safe. I'm not safe. Can you see why I'm not safe? *Come si brucia questa santa, cosi si brucera la mia anima.* Why I want out? Why I am out? *As burns this saint, so will burn my soul.* And you should get out too. Hey, you still got Bretlin to deal with."

Jules reacted to the name 'Bretlin' like she had been hit in the face with a ton of quarters.

"I can't protect you no more, Jules. You gotta go on your own. I can't keep watchin' out for ya."

I didn't want to look directly at Jules. I could tell she was upset; I glanced at her with the corners of my eyes. Tears.

"What should I do?" she asked Louie.

"Pay back the seventy-five hundred you owe Bretlin, maybe he'll forget how you sandbagged him."

Jules sat in silence. She was staring down at the sixteen lavender chips, the sixteen lavender chips that totaled eight thousand dollars.

"I know Bretlin, and he knows I know you. What he doesn't know is that I know where you live. I don't need for him to bring the Commission down harder on me just because he wants to get even with *you*. Do *me* a favor for a change, pay him back. Pay him back, stay away from me, and clean up. Stop the drugs, the partyin', the hookin', the stealin'."

"I steal for you."

"No more. Not you, not that nigger, nobody. We're all goin' straight."

"Jules going straight?" I had to say.

"Yeah, and you too, punk. I'm givin' ya boths a chance here."

"What's gonna happen to us, Louie, 'cause we fucked up?"

Louie thought about it for a long time but seemed to have already made up his mind. Again he went back and forth from Jules to me from Jules to me. He shook his head. "Nothin' if you get out now."

"What about K Dog? Anything gonna happen to K Dog?"

"You don't worry 'bout K Dog. I'll take care of—" Louie stopped himself. "Worry 'bout your selves," and then to Jules, "Pay back Bretlin." He glanced down at the lavender chips and gave a couple nods. "I can get the money to him and say it's from you. Do it if you know what's good for ya. For once, Jules, do somethin' right. Do somethin' right for a change in your life."

14

L ouie put us up at the Flamingo Hilton. He made a phone call
and arranged a complimentary deluxe suite for Jules and me
to spend the night if we promised to be out of town by noon
the next day which was Thursday, May 28. That was fine with me
because I needed to get back to work. Check-out was eleven a.m. If
we left then, we'd be back in L.A. by three-thirty or four p.m. I'd be
standing behind the bar at six handing Craig, Ed, and Harold their
usual on-the-way-home cocktails. But no, Jules had to be difficult.
She wanted to stay.

Fingers and Pumpkin Head dropped us off in front of the hotel.

"Remember, Louie wants you out of town by noon," Fingers said
as if he were the main man in control. "You better take his advice."

"Thanks for the ride," Jules said as she slammed the rear car door
in the middle of "You better—" And then she added, "Fuck face."

We picked up two card-keys from the Hotel Guests desk and rode
the elevator to the seventh floor. I couldn't help myself but to laugh
and mention to Jules that this whole thing with Louie and his
cowboys was like something out of a western movie—*"Be out of
town by noon, if you know what's good for ya, partner."* Jules didn't
say anything. She was quiet and nervous. I could tell she was
scheming something in that dangerous mind of hers.

As soon as we entered the deluxe suite—which was basically a
one bedroom apartment—Jules headed straight for the wet bar,
twist-opened a nipper bottle of Absolut vodka and downed it in one

swallow. She threw a nipper Tanqueray bottle to me. I walked into the kitchen, found a glass, tonic, some ice in the half-sized refrigerator and made myself a gin 'n' tonic.

Jules walked around inspecting our overnight palace. "Do you believe this?" she said, walking over to a large drapery spanning across the entire living area. She then drew the strings to allow the rest of the world in. Tiny twinkling lights flickered in the black distance. Kaleidoscopic lights from the Flamingo and neighboring casinos cast a distorted luminous glow onto the Colorado River below us.

Jules found Flamingo Hilton literature on a desk and started perusing it. I took a sip from my gin 'n' tonic. It tasted cool and refreshing. I peeked into the bedroom. A king-sized bed was centered in the room. I stood in the doorway. A rush of feeling lucky swept over me then vanished just as quickly.

Jules picked up and tossed down colorful brochures. I leaned against the doorjamb of the bedroom and contemplated where I was and why. I was content for the moment, relieved that I wouldn't be involved in the stealing of cars anymore.

"There's all kinds of shit to do around here," Jules proclaimed.

"Yeah, if you're a tourist. Speaking of which," I said as I pushed myself off the jamb, my contentedness now out the window, "what was that you said to Louie, 'Mickey and I'll get a place. You can hook us up with a couple jobs.' What the fuck was that all about?" It was on my mind to ask her ever since she had said it.

She ignored my question while studying another brochure, "Mmmm, 'InTouch' Massage, one-half hour and hour appointments. Available 'In-House.'"

"*Jules.*"

"*What?*"

"You think I want to *live* in *Laughlin?*"

"*I* want to live in Laughlin."

I pictured myself driving back to L.A. alone.

"I want to hang on to Louie, that's all," she blurted out, finally addressing her motivation.

"Stop relying on him. Get over it." I took a good swig of my drink and approached her, stopping a few steps behind her.

"I can't. He's been like a father to me."

"And like a father, he's telling you what to do. So maybe now you'll do what he says. Get a job like the rest of us working stiffs."

I crossed the room and peered out the window. A plane with its running lights was traveling low in the sky. I focused my eyes from the plane to the black glass of the window, which mirrored Jules, now the center of my attention.

Jules was not happy. "Well I thought maybe he'd help us get jobs here, get me—us—set up."

"I've got a job. But if I don't get back by tomorrow night, Dottie just might find someone else who wants it. What are you going to do here anyway? Cocktail waitress?"

"May-be." Jules said, beginning to pout.

"Hustle?" I sneered.

"I can make a hundred to two hundred grand a year," she answered as if I had just given her a new reason for her existence.

I turned around and faced her. "That's just great. Outside of the casino life there's nothing here. Nada. Zip. What if you and I start gambling? And liked it? Then what? What if we get fucking addicted to gambling? That's all we need. I don't need another fucking addiction." I crossed over to the television set and absentmindedly read television programming information printed on top of it. "Besides, it's not L.A. It's not what I'm after."

"What *are* you after?"

It was a good question. I knew deep down I wanted to get things out of me and onto paper and onto the screen. But I didn't say that; instead I said, "I need to stay in L.A., that's all."

"Why? When was the last time you wrote anything besides a check for rent, and do you even have the money for that?" She threw down a brochure about the Grand Canyon, turned and walked back over to the wet bar. "What the fuck?"

"If I keep hanging around with you, I'll end up writing from County Jail."

Jules let out a sarcastic "maybe you should try it sometime" while twisting open a nipper of Bacardi. She eyed me with contempt as she lifted the rum to her lips.

Twice that night Jules spoke the truth. She hit the old proverbial nail on the head. Never mind what would become of Jules, what would become of me?

I picked up the remote control for the television, clicked it on and surfed channels. "I'm going back tomorrow with or without you," I told Jules.

"Let's take this pretty color chip and win some money." She was admiring the lavender chip cupped in the small of her hand.

I didn't say anything. I was preparing for an argument. She wanted to stay in Laughlin and I was going to talk her out of it.

Jules finished off the bottle. "Well, I'm going downstairs with or without you," she said, imitating me; then she threw the empty bottle into a far corner wastebasket. Clunk. Three points. "I'm gonna cash in my chip." She put the chip back in her cut-off jeans pocket.

"Is it your chip or our chip? Is it your chip or mine and Bill's chip? Or is it K Dog's chip? Or is Louie going to smoke him so he won't even need a fucking chip?" I watched vignettes of television programs flash by, *chip, chip, chip, chip* ringing in my brain.

Jules walked towards me swinging her shoulders proudly. "Good thing I told Louie the truth about what really went down. I knew he knew. I had a feeling when those two goons were taking us to the boat that he knew. I wasn't going to take a chance and lie to Louie. We wouldn't be here now if I told him we walked in on the dead guy. We'd be at the *bottom* of Lake Mojave with the fucking trout—the fucking cutthroat trout—if there is such a fucking fish. Instead we're here at the *top* of the fucking Flamingo."

I stopped clicking the remote when I recognized a scene from the movie *Bonnie and Clyde*.

"What are we going to tell Bill and K?" I asked, calmer now.

"I don't know yet. We'll tell them we couldn't find Louie, or he decided not to pay for the cars because the mechanic got killed, or Louie wants to lay low, or something like that."

DANGEROUS LOVE

"How about telling them there was a fuck up with the money just like Louie said, except Louie never gave us the money and that he's going to get out of the business just like he also said. You're going to have to explain to Bill and K Dog why they're not stealing cars anymore. Whatever you come up with Louie's got to know so he can—"

"Look, the only person Louie talks to is me. He doesn't talk to Bill or K Dog about anything. I'm the only one, so anything I say Bill and K Dog will have to believe."

I turned up the volume on the television and sat at the edge of a plush two-seat couch. The scene when Bonnie was visiting her mother and family in Texas was on. It's an emotional scene in the movie for Bonnie. She hadn't seen her "mama" in a long time—and it would be the last time. Bonnie and Clyde had by this time racked up quite a reputation for robbing banks and killing people.

Jules sat down in a chair to my left. We both watched the movie. I wondered if Jules was thinking about her own mother during this scene, but she didn't let on if she was.

"Maybe that's what we should do," Jules said.

"What?"

"Rob banks."

"That's brilliant. That's really a brilliant idea. That's all we need to do next. Let's just go do that right now."

"Why can't we be like them?"

I looked at her like she was crazy. "*Them* got killed, remember?"

In the movie someone asked where Clyde was headed to...

Clyde just answered that they weren't headed nowhere, they were jus' runnin' from.

"How much stuff we have left?" Jules asked.

"I don't know... should go get the car anyway, everything's in the car."

"Go get the car, get the stash and our bags, we'll clean up and then go win some money."

"If we lose, we have nothing, less than what we came with, fucking worthless."

"Did you ever think we might win?"

"We're not gonna win. We're losers. We're nothin' but a bunch of fuckin' losers."

I clicked the movie off after Clyde said to Bonnie that he was better at running than he was at robbing banks.

We sat there and stared at the dark blank screen. I took the last gulp of my drink, *losers* chiming in my head. Jules was pouting. I was thinking.

Then I changed my mind. "Okay, what's the fucking difference," I succumbed, "we cash in the chip fifty-fifty together. I take my two-fifty and do what I want with it. I gamble what I want to gamble. You take your two-fifty and do what you want with it."

"Fine, two-fifty, two-fifty."

I went to get the car.

When I got back Jules was gone.

I couldn't come up with one good idea of where Jules could have disappeared. Maybe she went to get ice. But there was plenty of ice in the refrigerator's freezer. Maybe she went downstairs to use a pay phone because she didn't want to use the one in the room for some reason. Maybe this... Maybe that... Maybe she just left and wasn't coming back.

I took a personal inventory of how much money I had in my life at that moment. I went through my pockets and counted out one hundred thirty-three dollars. I tried to remember what I had in my bank account. I had seven hundred eighty-three dollars to my name. I added the split from the lavender chip. And it was the end of the month. I had June rent to pay in four days. Maybe a little gambling was my only hope. What if God directed all my actions in my life in order for me to end up in Nevada at that moment in time so I could drop three silver quarters into the Magic Million Dollar Go-Around slot machine and win a million bucks. I didn't think so. I don't think God works that way.

At least I had the drugs. I opened the Hide-a-Key container and was relieved to see two white crosses and a little less than one gram of crank. Jules and I had done quite a bit of the eight ball until the time

Fingers and Pumpkin Head frisked us and threw what remained into the lake.

The best thing would have been to get a good night's rest. I had been up for too many hours now to count; but no way was I the least bit tired. Maybe if I didn't do an upper I'd still be able to get a few hours sleep before we—or *I*—hit the road.

I swallowed half of a white cross with a new Tanqueray 'n' tonic.

I took a shower.

Time crept by.

No Jules.

"...Probably cashed in the chip and is blowing the entire five hundred right now," I said out loud to the face in the bathroom mirror.

I went downstairs and strolled the casino both looking for her and absorbing the action. Gamblers were clamoring around some of the Flamingo's specialty games: Let It Ride, Caribbean Stud, Pai Gow Poker and Spanish 21. I looked in restaurants, bars, lounges, outside, everywhere. I walked to the Riverside and then the Regency looking for her. I went back to the Flamingo and called the room. No answer.

I changed a ten dollar bill into forty quarters. I sat down in front of a slot machine and started filling its contents. I won a few dollars; I lost a few dollars. A pretty cocktail waitress approached me. I ordered another gin. So that's what Jules wants to do? Cocktail waitress and hook on the side... or was it the other way around? Then it dawned on me. Maybe she was out making money, but not from gambling. Maybe she was out selling blow jobs, letting men fuck her, letting them fuck her up the ass, *that'll be another two hundred dollars for that, sir.* I could just see it now. It made me furious. I stood up and stepped away from the Carnival of Fortune slot machine that had paid me back twenty-nine dollars in profit. At least I was twenty-nine dollars ahead. I wasn't losing. I was winning. But that didn't make me feel any better.

I called the room again. Still no answer.

I thought of *The Getaway* with Steve McQueen and Ali MacGraw when they stole hundreds of thousands of dollars and escaped to Mexico.

I went back to the room and opened the door half-expecting, half-hoping Jules would be there. She wasn't.

I walked over to the window and stared out. The earth and sky were discernable. Again, I greeted a new day with open eyes.

Okay, if that's the way it was going to be.

I packed my bag. I was going to teach Jules a lesson and leave without her. Revenge percolated my veins. I couldn't wait to get out of there now. I couldn't leave fast enough so Jules would walk in after a night of whoring and see that I was gone. That I dissed her. That I was the one in control.

Then I heard the swiping of a card-key. The disengagement of metal from metal, the opening of a heavy door.

Jules stumbled in—her perfect body a wreck.

She slammed the door behind herself muttering fucking this and fucking thats…

Her face wasn't pretty anymore; it was contorted, ugly, bruised. Midnight Oasis Eye shadow was dripping down her cheeks and congealed with the coagulation of the black and blue and purple puffiness on the right side of her face. She hadn't been slapped. She had been hit, brutally, not only on her face but her entire body.

Jules stumbled over to the refrigerator and pulled out an ice cube tray. Ice cubes fell to the floor. The ones that didn't she held to her face.

I stood there with my bag in hand. I was bewildered. Scenarios ran through my mind, and before I could say anything Jules asked in a soft innocuous whisper, "Where you going?"

"I didn't think you were coming back."

Jules didn't say anything. She slumped to the kitchen floor and ached.

I dropped my bag, neared her slowly, and bent down to her level. I didn't ask what happened or where she'd been. Instead, I sat down next to her and swaddled her in my arms. Hot tears melted the ice.

And that's the way we fell asleep.

15

I awoke disoriented and confused by the pounding sound of a fat fist rattling a door. I was sitting on a floor leaning against a cabinet in a kitchen somewhere. Lying on the floor in a fetal position in front of me a woman moved ever so slightly. The woman picked her head up and moaned something indistinguishable. Oh, yeah, then I remembered, I was in a hotel in Laughlin, Nevada, with hell-bent crazy Jules. I tried hard to remember what day it was. More pounding. "OKAY!" I shouted. I crept up, panicked, and opened the door.

A large man dressed in a dark suit stood in the hallway.

"Y-e-a-h?" I was barely able to get out.

"Check-out's at eleven. It's eleven-thirty. Do you plan on staying or leaving?"

"Leaving."

"Good." I must have looked like shit because then he asked me, "Is everything okay?"

"Yeah, everything's fine. We'll be outta here in ten minutes."

The suit walked away. It was a blur now.

I closed the door. "Jules… Jules."

A barely audible sound came from the kitchen floor.

"We gotta go," I said.

I slowly walked over to her. I stood there and watched her do nothing. She wasn't moving. She looked dead.

"JULES!"

147

The dead woman's body moved.

"We gotta go. Now."

"All right, all right. What day is it?"

"I think it's Thursday. But it's eleven-thirty. We have to be out of here."

"Day or night?"

"Day."

"Call room service."

"We don't have time for room service."

"Room service!" Jules yelled out and rolled around on the floor.

"I'm sorry, sir," the woman on the other side of the line of room service said, "but you're already checked out."

I hung up the phone and gave Jules the bad news.

"Fuck them," she said.

"No, fuck us. We'll get coffee and donuts on the way out of town," I said, things coming back to me.

"I'm not going."

"We can't stay here."

"I need to call Louie."

"No, you don't need to call Louie. C'mon, let's go."

I tried to help her up. She wouldn't let me. She shrugged me off.

"I need a hit. Do we have anything left?" she asked, now sitting up. Her hair was a mess, her face swollen and ugly. Dried blood stained her clothes.

I gave her the second half of the white cross I had taken earlier. I then swallowed the last one. We inhaled two blasts each of crank leaving enough for me to get through the rest of the day and night. I made up my mind Jules wasn't getting any more. I needed more than she did; after all, I had to drive three hundred miles and get through a night of work. We were both moving in slow motion, but after ten minutes when the crank took effect, we were wired again.

Jules sat on the bed. "I need to smoke a bunch of assholes before we leave."

"Do you want to tell me what happened?"

I stood there and waited for Jules to tell me who she was going to

148

kill and why. She reached for the phone on the end table next to the bed. She picked up the handset and sat there.

"What's the matter?" I asked.

"I don't know his number."

"You're calling Louie?"

"Well, obviously not. We gotta go out there."

"No way."

"I gotta see Louie."

"Why, you think he's going to help you take care of whoever did this to you?"

"Yeah, he'll do it. He'll do anything I say."

"He told you last night he doesn't want anything to do with you anymore. He told you, you were trouble. He's fed up with you."

"When he sees these bruises he'll help me."

"Look, I'm sorry, but I don't think I can take this anymore. Louie and everybody's right. You're nothing but trouble. You leave the room without waiting for me, you get yourself beat up and you won't tell me why, a goon comes to the door making sure we're out of here…"

"Who was at the door?"

"One of Louie's wranglers, I'm sure. He's probably down the hall or in the lobby waiting to escort us out of town, who the fuck knows? Now, are you coming back to L.A. with me or not?"

"I need a cigarette." Jules fumbled through her belongings for a cigarette.

"Do you want to go to the police?"

"Fuck the police."

"Okay. Do you at least want to tell me what happened?"

Jules ignored my interrogation. She sat on the bed still holding the phone and lit a cigarette, her eyes riveted into an open space somewhere across the room.

"What happened to the chip?" I asked.

Jules dropped her head into her hands.

Again I asked, "Do you still have the chip?"

"No."

I didn't press the issue. Instead, I picked up my bag. "All right. Let me put it to you this way. I'm going back to L.A. right now. You can stay or you can come with me, which is it?"

I waited for ten seconds for an answer. There was none. I walked out the door.

Jules came running out of the room and followed me down the hallway to the elevator.

The time was twelve-o-five.

My head was pounding. Jules was a mumbling mess. The crank hadn't helped that much. It only brought us back to where we were—nowhere. I thought of Warren Beatty, Faye Dunaway, Steve McQueen, and Ali McGraw.

We needed to eat. I stopped for donuts and coffee, my head still in a whirl.

I filled the Mustang with low-leaded gasoline.

Traffic congestion on Needles Highway stopped us for some reason I cannot remember.

By the time we got on I-40, I was beginning to feel the sparseness of life. It was twelve forty-five. A vast desert loomed in front of us. Clouds gathered adding grayness to the landscape. Slow bluesy guitars licked an open air from a radio station somewhere hidden in the ethereals of a distant space.

The Smithereens sang, "Too Much Passion."

Coyotes in the distant mountains turned their heads. Wind-blown tumbleweeds scattered their seed. Rattlesnakes slept hidden in crevices. Prairie dogs scuttled into their holes. Lizards scattered and scorpions crawled. Grasshoppers leaped. Joshua trees stood their ground. The scent of sagebrush lingered in the arid air. Mimosa clustered far away. Cactus tolerated their spinescent existence.

It started to rain—hard. I pulled over to put up the top. Thunder shattered my nerves and lightning took both our breaths away. Rain like marbles pelted the Mustang.

There is an Almighty.

I tried to drive but couldn't see five feet in front of us. I pulled the car over again.

We were only twenty minutes outside of Laughlin.

"This is crunching my time," I said in frustration.

We were silent. I wondered if a flash flood would carry us back to Laughlin. Was I cursed and doomed to never leave there? The rain smashed the car harder, bullets of raindrops shooting into the polyvinyl convertible top. Thunder and lightning exploded directly overhead. Then, it started to hail.

We sat there, helpless, the motor running.

Jules was aching.

I lit a Marlboro and thought about what the Marlboro Man would do in a situation like this. He'd find a wooded area and light a cigarette waiting, too, for the storm to subside.

I was expecting hail to shatter the windshield any second.

An awkward silence between Jules and me shrouded us up to that point in the return trip. I looked over at Jules and in the calmest voice I could whisper I asked her again what happened. She told me.

❊   ❊   ❊

"I went downstairs to get cigarettes. I was going to go back to the room, but I figured it was going to take you some time to go find the car and come back. So I had a drink at the bar. There were a couple guys there. Nothing special to look at, in their early twenties, so I thought at first. They kept looking at me. They whispered something between them. I knew it was about me. I could tell by the way they kept staring at me. Laughing. Drinking their stupid beers.

"One of them comes over to me... asks me if he can buy me a drink—even though I have a practically full glass already, the fucking asshole. But I said 'Sure, why not,' spend your money on me, fuck face.

"He sits down and starts bullshitting me, asking me questions... Am I from around here? Where am I from? What was I doing at the casino this late by myself? Who am I with? Do I have any friends 'in these parts,' he says.

"I told him I was from San Francisco, that I was waiting for someone and that we were going to pull some slots, maybe win some money and that yes, I had some friends 'in these parts' some very important friends, I said. He said, 'Oh really, where are they?' I said it was none of his business.

"So he waves his friend over and his friend is standing between us with his beer in his hand and a smile on his face kinda goofy looking. And I'm looking at the both of them trying to figure out how old they really are because I swear they sure as hell didn't look old enough to be drinking beer in a casino.

"Now we're shooting the shit and now I want to leave. But the first guy—his name is Bobby—says I didn't get the drink he bought me. I told him that's okay I've got to go meet my friend—which incidentally is you of course. The other guy standing and smiling like an asshole moves in and says in a low voice, 'Hey, you wanna make a quick hundred before you go meet your friend?' I said – already knowing by the way he was looking at me up and down and smiling that fucked-up sick smile what he was after –I said, no thanks I gotta go. But then the other kid says, 'How about two hundred? Both of us? One hundred each?' Fifteen minutes each and that I'll be just a few minutes late in meeting up with my friend, but it'll be worth it because I'd be making two hundred dollars in about a half-hour. I'm figuring now with these kids probably three minutes each—and I know *we* can use the money and that you probably wouldn't mind if I gave you a hundred out of it."

"Like the money you split with me from the guy at the beach?"

"I didn't give you the split?"

"Never mind, go on."

"What are you talking about?"

"You never gave me the split; go on, tell me the rest of your story."

"So anyway I told them they'd have to give me the money first. They said okay and we walk to the Flamingo's parking lot. My plan was to get the money from them before I got into the car and then run screaming my bloody head off rape.

"We get to the car except it's not a car, it's a van, a brand new van—I don't know what kind but it was sparkling new. I said, 'You have to give me the money first.' Bobby says okay and reaches into his pocket and counts out a hundred dollars in small bills. I said, 'Jesus c'mon, man.' At the same time his friend, I don't know his name, opens the driver's side door and gets in behind the wheel. I said, 'Where's the other hundred?' This asshole Bobby said that's his half, opened the side door, grabs me by the arm and shoves me into the rear of the van. He then jumps in back with me and slides the door shut. The driver takes off screeching the tires before I could try to jump out. The guy in back with me says that we're just going to drive around and then *Ronny* is going to get in the back and have his turn. I told them I wasn't going anywhere with them and for them to turn around and bring me back. They laughed. This kid Ronny the driver—the smiler—he laughed and said, 'We ain't bringin' you back,' and sped up with a look of glory on his face. I thought again of jumping out, but already we were going too fast.

"Anyway, the inside of the van is under some kind of construction like these guys are making it some kind of a pleasure fucking vehicle with a fucking mattress and shelves and shit... and this guy in back with me ties my hands to the back legs of the front seats. While he's unzipping his fly he's telling me that yeah they got some friends I might want to meet. I told them I'd give them their money back if they brought me back. Bobby told me, oh, he'd be getting his money back anyway. And this fucking Ronny kid is looking in the rear view mirror and turning around and giving me his shitty grin.

"This guy I'm in the back with tries to stick his cock into my mouth but I'm keeping my mouth shut turning my head from side to side. He slaps me across the face and tells me to take it. So I open my mouth and take him, then you know what I do?"

"What do you do?"

"I bite hard and I'm not letting go."

I winced. I cupped my crotch with my hands and imagined what it would be like. "You gotta be kidding me."

"That's when he lets me have it the first time. He punches my ear.

He punched me so hard that his cock fell out of my mouth. Then he started walloping my head, my ears, my face. He takes my jeans off and tries to stick his cock up me, except he's hurting so much he can't. His driver friend kept asking him if he was okay and Bobby kept saying no, how it hurt, and the goof-ball driving just kept asking if he was okay. What an asshole.

"This guy gets off of me and starts to check out his cock and feeling it and he's got blood on his hands. I wished I had a gun.

"So we're driving for about another five minutes and I'm on the fucking floor wondering how the hell I'm going to get out of this and if they'd just throw me out of the van I'd be happy.

" 'You're a fucking dead girl now,' this guy Bobby says, 'we're gonna fucking bury you,' and he's crying 'cause his cock is hurting him so much.

"So now we turn and I look up and what I see is a neon sign that says 'Bull Ranch Bar' only these guys think I don't see the name of the place because I don't think I'm supposed to know where I am.

"They drive in what I think is the back of this shit-kicking real cowboy's bar and the driver gets out and goes inside and comes out with two other guys—a little older looking—one's wearing a fucking cowboy hat. They're all standing crowded around the open door looking at me and this dumb-ass Ron guy tells them what happened about Bobby almost getting his cock bitten off. The two guys crack up laughing except Bobby who is still hurting and moaning about how he's going to have to see a doctor and maybe a *nurse* is going to have to look at it. He's pulling his jeans up and climbing all hurt like out of the van.

"Things weren't so funny now. The other two guys asked where'd they find me and Ron just told the whole story like it happened, proud and shit. Bobby walks into the rear entrance of the bar and disappears. The other two guys they get in the back, tell Ron to look out and slide the door shut. I scream for help. They tied a bandana over my mouth.

"Then they raped me," Jules said, tears streaming down her blood-dried cheeks.

"They both just kept raping me and raping me.

"Bobby comes back opens the door and says, 'We're gonna kill this bitch. We already got a hole dug in the desert for you,' he said to me. 'Give me my money back, bitch,' he says, fumbling through the pockets of my shorts. He finds his money and the chip. 'What's this?' he goes, 'five-hundred bucks!' He's all happy now.

"The guy with the cowboy hat tells him to shut up and that nobody was going to hurt me. They just want to have some *fun*. After they were done with me they told Ron and Bobby to get lost. Ronny complained that he hadn't gotten any. The dorky cowboy hat guy said, 'Too bad.' He was the oldest and obviously the one in control.

"He tells his friend to get in the driver's seat and drive. Well fucking this Ronny guy starts shouting and these other two guys just take the van and drive away. They drive for about five minutes. Cowboy hat guy unties me. The van stops, he slides the door open and kicks me out. Then he throws my clothes out on top of me and shit. They told me they had fun and thanks. They speed off. I knelt on the ground and started to cry on the edge of the road. I was cold. I put my clothes on. Then a car pulled over from the opposite direction. It was a nice married couple. I told them I had a fight with my boyfriend and that he threw me out of the car on our way back to Phoenix. They felt sorry for me and drove me back to the Flamingo even though they had just come from Laughlin because they both worked at Harrah's. The wife was a dealer and he was a cook."

I sat there nauseated. I felt sorry for Jules. Sure, she had it coming to her, but not that way. I had tied her up too, and fucked her all kinds of which ways, but that was different. That was *way* different.

The thunder and lightning and rain continued. Jules sniffled, rubbing the tears away with her delicate fingers.

"This is what I get," she told herself.

"I'm sorry," I said.

"Just drive, let's get out of here," Jules said, crying.

"No, let's go back. Let's get the motherfuckers who did this to you."

"What?" She looked at me as though she couldn't believe I had said that.

"Yeah, let's fuck them up."

❁   ❁   ❁

Jules and I talked for a while and came up with a plan. After the rain subsided I took the next exit and headed east for Bull Head City.

I bought a liter bottle of Bacardi's 151 rum while Jules went to ask someone where the Bull Ranch Bar was located and got directions. We drank a few good swigs from the bottle. Jules then ripped a T-shirt of mine, soaked it with rum and crammed parts of the T-shirt into the bottle—we made a Molotov Cocktail.

We found the bar. I drove into the rear parking lot while Jules ducked down in her seat. A van was parked in back.

Jules crept up and immediately recognized the van. "Yeah, that's it."

For once we were lucky. In a gambling town, we were lucky.

I looked for a security camera like the one at McDee's—and South Bay Auto Repair—and didn't see one. Jules lit the rum-soaked T-shirt with her lighter and threw the bottle hard on the ground underneath the van's gasoline tank. The bottle broke, sending flames up beneath the gas tank. We sped off.

About one minute later we heard an explosion. We both looked back and saw clouds of thick black smoke rising from behind the Bull Ranch Bar.

Jules whooped and hollered. I had never seen her so happy. She hugged and kissed me and her pain seemed to immediately disappear.

We drove back to Los Angeles, my eyes riveted to the rearview mirror.

"Have you thought out what you're going to tell the guys?" I asked Jules as she was climbing out of my car in front of her house.

"I'll think of something."

"Tell them Louie wouldn't give us the money because we fucked up. This'll clear us with the money *you* gave back to Louie to give to this Bretlin guy of yours. Then tell them the truth, Louie's out of business—just like he said he is. Go with this, okay? So if Bill and K Dog decide to ask me or if it comes up in conversation someday our stories will jive."

"What about my face? The bruises?"

"Tell them… tell them Louie's cowboys did it to you to teach you a lesson about not fucking up…."

"I don't have to say anything…"

"Yeah, you do, because then they'll think I did this to you. Tell them he wanted to teach you a lesson. Remember, one of his own got killed because of us. You took the beating for K Dog. I'm sure he'll appreciate that."

"What about you? How come they didn't beat you?"

"They did. They punched me in the stomach and kicked me in the balls a bunch of times. Bill and K Dog will know this is all it takes."

Jules kissed me and stepped out of the car. "Thanks for doing what you did today. I love you."

I nodded with a curt smile, "Take care of yourself. Get some rest."

I walked into McDee's a half-hour late. I made my apology to Karen. I counted my drawer and refilled Craig's, Ed's, and Harold's usuals.

Harold said, " 'Bout time you got here."

I couldn't be angry with Harold. Not this time.

16

A week had gone by since I'd seen or spoken with Jules. Though I needed a break from her, I spent many hours thinking about her. Yes, she was dangerous, but my curiosity and lust for her continued without restraint. I thought of calling her many times but let it go.

The flutter of a butterfly's wings brought us back together.

The following Friday night Jules walked into McDee's through the front door, which no one ever uses unless they're traveling on foot or by bus or they've been hitchhiking and got let off. This reminded me of Stephanie hitchhiking and how she "worked" Sepulveda and Victory Boulevards. She'd put her thumb out, get picked up by a strange guy, give him a blow job for fifty bucks while he drove around, then he'd let her off at one of a half-dozen bars in the area, where she would go in, purchase a shot of Peppermint Schnapps, rinse her mouth out from cum, have another shot, and go out and hitch a john again.

Peter stopped Jules and the two engaged themselves in hushed-toned conversation.

I looked at Charlene, who was sitting in her customary seat at the end of the bar, the empty spaces all filled in the *Los Angeles Times Crossword Puzzle*. Charlene noticed Jules, looked at me and shrugged her shoulders.

I moved over to Charlene. She knew what I was going to ask.

"Dottie said it was okay," Charlene confirmed.

"Why didn't she tell me?"

"I was supposed to… I forgot," Charlene said and laughed, "but she can only have three drinks and I'm supposed to watch her," Charlene added rolling her eyes, "like I'm her baby sitter or something."

"You're gonna watch her?"

"No, you are." And then she laughed again.

Jamie, who was sitting alone at the bar, tossed her long blonde hair back, took a deep drag from her Marlboro Light and blew out a long stream of gray-blue smoke. "What is *she* doing here?" she asked me when I started pacing.

"Dottie let her back in," I said.

"This should be interesting."

We all rolled our eyes. Jamie smirked. We knew with Jules back in the bar there was sure to be trouble, eventually, sometime down the line.

Jules looked at me and gave me a smile that said *surprise!* I nodded and forced a smile. A giant knot formed in my stomach. I needed a cigarette, a drink, and a hit.

She and Peter broke away from each other. I didn't notice if a transaction took place or not and really didn't care one way or the other if there had been. Jules made her way to the bar, which still had a few seats available since it was early in the evening. She sat down a few stools from Jamie and said "Hi" to me and Charlene. She either didn't see Jamie or ignored her. Jamie kept quiet.

Jules's bruises were fading but still noticeable under foundation makeup if one were to look close in the dim light.

"What happened to your face?" Charlene asked genuinely concerned.

"Got into a fight with my roommate, Stephanie," Jules lied to Charlene.

"Who won?" Charlene asked.

"I did, of course," she said to Charlene, then to me she said, "I had a talk with Dottie. She said it was okay for me to come back in."

"Yeah, I know," I said.

"Three drink max," den mother Charlene said.

"Does a shot of gold and a Corona chaser count as one or two?" Charlene laughed.

"C'mon, Jules, two," I said and chuckled a little myself.

"What about a *double* shot of gold and a Corona?"

"Don't push it, but I'll let that go by as two," I said as I opened and poured.

"No wonder I love you so much." Jules got all comfy at the bar with her tequila and beer and lit a Newport. She pulled out a handful of bills and put a C-note on the bar.

I wanted to know what she had told Bill and K Dog about Louie and Laughlin, so I looked straight into her eyes and hinted, "How's *everything*? I thought of calling you a few times."

She picked up on it. "Everything's fine, but our phone got disconnected on Monday."

"How much do you owe?"

"Over three hundred."

"You're in hell with Pacific Bell."

"Yeah, with P.G. and E. too... electricity and gas got shut off today," Jules said almost proudly.

I leaned in. I picked up the C-note, snapped it between my thumb and middle finger and held the bill up to her, "You know, if you just give these people a call they'll usually let you slide... make an arrangement to pay... you have to show them you're making an effort... even if it's only a few dollars a month." I turned, rang the sale, and made change. Jules took a swig of her Cuervo like she didn't care.

I laid down ninety-two dollars in front of her.

"Do you have any candles I can borrow?" she asked me.

"How do you *borrow* candles? Is that like borrowing a cigarette?" I tried to make a joke but it came out more sarcastic than I wanted it to.

I heard Jamie stifle a laugh.

"Okay, do you have any candles I can *have*?"

"Sure, you can have some candles."

"Thanks." And before I could suggest again that she get a job and get on with her life as a normal human being she said, "I think I gotta job."

"Where?"

"Dancing," she answered the 'where' question with a 'what' answer.

"Dancing?"

"Cat's Meow. I should know in a couple days when I start."

I felt Jamie roll her eyes again.

I didn't let on that I knew from Peter that she had already once worked there.

"You can practically walk there," I said.

"Practically." She said 'practically' like there was no chance in hell she was going to walk the five or six blocks it would take to get there.

(None of us knew what had happened to the Datsun. It disappeared one day.)

"Is Bones here?" she asked looking around.

"Bones got busted."

"Again?"

"He was pulled over on Coldwater and Sherman Way the other night for running a *yellow* light. They searched him. He was holding seventeen vials."

"What's this, his third time?"

"Something like that."

"Did he make bail?"

"Of course; you know Bones. But no one's seen him since. Why, you want something?"

"No," she said, "not really."

Not really? Was that like I want to borrow *some candles?*

Jules knew she could get something from someone—Jamie or Charlene—but she probably didn't feel comfortable asking them yet this early in the game after having the privilege of just being allowed in McDee's again. Obviously, Peter didn't have anything.

We small-talked for a while about this and that, stupid stuff, where Stephanie was—she moved out and was living with some guy at his apartment in Hollywood.

Jules finished her beer. "Gotta go."

"Do you want to come over tonight?" I asked her without thinking. "I've got electricity."

"Will you turn *me* on?" she said as if I had made her day.

"You know I will."

"Then I'll be over," she said suddenly a little happier with the world.

"C'mon back at closing."

"Okay," she said as she jumped off her chair, said "Goodbye" to Charlene and me and bounced towards the front door, "See ya!" and walked out into the orange sunlight. She left me a five dollar tip.

She reminded me of the night I first met her—the way I wanted her. I didn't know why I still wanted her and didn't care how much trouble she was.

JAMIE
You're still going out with her, huh…

ME
We're making a movie together.

CHARLENE
Must be a thriller.

We all shared a good laugh over that one.

Jules came back to the bar later that night, surprisingly straight and sober. We went to my place. We fucked on the bed. Then we watched television. I held her in my arms. We talked about both of us going straight, not drinking anymore—at least not as much—how we were ruining our lives, how we vowed to be better to ourselves. That was the way we fell asleep, dreaming dreams of untruths.

The next night Jules came into McDee's with K Dog. K Dog had never been in McDee's. He slowly walked up to the bar cool and casual and gave me a big smile.

K Dog never smiled. I never saw his meticulous white and perfect teeth.

I knew why they were there. Since Bones, the kingpin dealer of McDee's would be lying low, Jules figured they would be able to move in on his territory. All the other dealers like Charlene and Jamie were small time and didn't have the weight Bones had.

K Dog knew this and was willing to be Jules's silent supplier— her executive producer. He was there to investigate his potential investment.

Dottie happened to have been sitting at the bar that early Saturday night. She of course noticed Jules and K Dog and then looked at me—not with a discerning eye but just a look. K Dog ordered a gin 'n' juice for himself and a Corona for Jules.

Jules went over to Dottie and schmoozed Dottie, making her laugh a lot. Jules was good at putting on the political charm when she needed to.

"What's up?" I asked K Dog.

"Jus' kickin'."

The last time I saw K Dog we had stolen cars together and I witnessed him killing a man. I tried to be at ease.

"Lights are out at Jules's, she tells me," I said to him.

"Skank pussy ain't cool."

Was there dissension? "What do you mean?" I asked.

"Bitch got people comin' over all hours of the night… shiiit… she fucked up, dude." K Dog took a giant chug from his drink. "I'll have another." He took out a wad of bills and handed me a twenty. I assumed he was paying for Jules.

I made another gin and juice for K Dog.

"Thanks, yo. Keep the change." K Dog watched me work while sipping on his drink. "You all right." Then he looked at Jules who was still at work charming Dottie.

"That the boss lady?" he asked me in a low tone.

I nodded the affirmative.

"You know everybody in here, right?"

"Mostly."

K Dog was scheming. He was being cool, small talk mostly and just looking around with his eyes, not moving his head much, not making any sudden movements, slow, calculating.

Jules walked over.

"Let's go girl, we be outta here," K Dog said.

"I didn't finish my beer."

"Got plenty o' beer in the car," K Dog said to Jules, then to me, "Thanks again yo."

They were gone.

                    DOTTIE
She's a spitfire that one, hey Mickey?

                     ME
Can't seem to douse her out.

                    DOTTIE
Who was that with her?

                     ME
I don't know, I never saw him before.

Later, I found out from Charlene that Dottie didn't know anything *yet* about Jules and me "going out." Dottie would find out eventually. She'd find out about everything. Somehow these "everythings" leak out and get around—like rumors and gossips.

❀   ❀   ❀

Los Angeles Times, June 8, 1992 – In the latest response to Willie Williams taking over Police Chief Daryl F. Gates's job, Gates was quoted as saying, "I said I was going to retire at the end of June and my feeling is now, screw you. I'll retire when I want to retire."... Seismic experts are concerned about an active fault in the Pacific

Ocean less than two miles from the Malibu Pier, further study has fallen on deaf ears… A truce-inspired barbecue for gang members at a Watts housing project ended in a brawl when police tried to break up the party and were mobbed by angry blacks…

❖   ❖   ❖

On June 10, when I walked in to start my workweek and Wednesday shift, Jules was there. Madonna was singing "Vogue" on the jukebox. The usual suspects were in attendance.

"You have to do something about your girlfriend," Karen said to me while I was dropping my drawer into the register, "she's high on something."

"How many drinks did she have?" I asked Karen as I looked into the mirror and saw Jules's reflection. She was dancing and striking poses in front of some guy I had never seen before who was sitting at a booth near the pool table.

"Two margaritas. But she's been here since one and you don't get that high from nursing two drinks in five hours… keeps going into the ladies room. I think she's dealing, too. I'm not going to put up with her, Mickey. I'll have Dottie eighty-six her again."

Dottie was already gone for the day, so it was up to me now to take care of things.

"Guess what?" Jules said to me after Madonna faded away and there was a slice of peace between songs, "We got our final eviction notice. We have to be out of there by yesterday."

"Where you gonna go?"

Jules shrugged her shoulders, stumbled a bit and said, "Don't know, don't care, margarita."

"I don't think so Jules, you're stumbling."

"No, I'm not."

"Yeah, you are."

"Then I'll go somewhere else," Jules said and pirouetted, ricocheting off chairs and tables.

Craig looked down at his rum 'n' Coke and shook his head. Ed took a sip of his Southern Comfort on the rocks. Harold had an angry face. Gary gently tapped the cue ball which tapped the nine ball, missing the shot. Jamie readied her shot at the six ball, smirking, shaking her head, looking in Jules's direction, and then playing her shot. Peter Gabriel's "Shock the Monkey," filled the air. The guy at the booth got up and walked over to Jules, said something in her ear and took her by the arm. Jules pulled herself away from him.

"I'll be fine," she said to the guy, who backed off.

Jules stumbled to the front door and opened it. A thick ray of sunlight blasted through the open door reminding us all there was a world outside from that dark and dank cellar of hell.

"I'll be back," was her final promise to us all.

Everybody made comments on Jules's condition and talked about how much of a drug addict and slut she was.

I hated everyone at that moment. They were such hypocrites. We all had problems.

❁　❁　❁

Peter was the one who found out first. Bill called him from Van Nuys Jail. Jules wasn't home at the time it all went down at nine o'clock in the morning on Friday, June 12. She was staying over at my place. Bill was the only one home. He was sleeping when the banging at the door started, when the Los Angeles Police Department and the Drug Enforcement Administration arrived in full regalia to search the premises for "drugs and drug paraphernalia with intent to sell," when they turned everything upside down, opened all the cabinets and drawers in the entire house, when they tore cereal boxes, threw clothes in the air, lifted toilet tank covers, ripped apart videocassettes, overturned mattresses, took pictures off the walls, ravaged through the medicine cabinet, confiscated the answering machine, wrecked havoc on dying plants, broke radios and a brand new Sony television set and a Sanyo CD player, and finally, *finally* finding what they were looking for in a large red auto mechanic's Craftsman tool box in a far corner of the garage: two ounces of powder cocaine, one ounce of fentanyl citrate ("China White" heroin), almost two ounces of crystallized metamphetamine ("Ice"), two-point-two kilograms of "Maui-Waui" marijuana, a gram/ounce scale, plastic bags, measuring spoons, all kinds of paraphernalia, and, *and*, an accounting ledger containing all purchases, sales and transactions of... well, drugs. The entries were written in Bill's handwriting; Bill Pacht, whose name was on the lease for renting out the house; Bill, who already had an outstanding warrant for his arrest from a San Francisco court for jumping bail on a previous charge of drug dealing and trafficking; Bill who was now basically going to prison for a long, long time.

Bill, who was asked if he knew where a Joanne Luchenski of Chicago of Milwaukee of Las Vegas, a.k.a. Julina Lukens, could be located; Ms. Luchenski, who was once convicted on a concealed weapons charge; Ms. Luchenski, who spent time recently at Sybil Brand County Jail for Women for a first offense of Grand Theft Auto; who was supposed to check in with her parole officer from time to time, but seemed to have missed the last fourteen appointments; Ms. Luchenski, who is being sought for the questioning of an attempted murder on one Jimi Sanchez in Panorama City on the night of Tuesday, April 21 in the year of our Lord 1992.

"Are you arresting me?" Bill asked Sergeant Taylor of the Van Nuys Division.

"Yes, son, we're arresting you."

"What about my Miranda Rights and an attorney?"

Sergeant Taylor recited the Miranda Rights to Bill, who then remained silent.

17

Ever since the rape and car bombing incidents in Laughlin, Jules and I had been getting along. Disaster does bring people closer together. We didn't argue much—like we were accustomed to anyway—and I felt we were making love more than we were fucking. That was why when Jules's phone, electricity, and gas got shut off, and the inevitable consequence that she and Bill were going to get evicted, I let her stay with me. Already she had most of her clothes cramping my closet and was practically moved in anyway. We would stay up for days and nights partying and making love.

The LAPD and DEA had been watching Bill's and Jules's "activities" for six months—standard modus operandi for a drug bust. The search and seizure coincided with an annual routine drug sweep. In a Los Angeles "drug sweep," a section of L.A., this particular time Van Nuys, individual daily and nightly swarms of local police and federal Drug Enforcement Administration agents converged on suspected drug dealers—those who sold large quantities out of apartments and houses. Helicopters with SX-16 Nitesun 30-million candle power search beams hovered above while doors were knocked down, guns wielded, babies cried, sirens blared, girlfriends shouted, drugs confiscated, paraphernalia overturned, arrests made, bondsmen called, jails filled.

INTERIOR—MICKEY'S APARTMENT—NIGHT

Jules was on the lam. I let her stay with me until "things blew over" as Jules put it.

"How are they going to blow over? They'll look for you until they find you," I told her, "maybe you should've stayed in Laughlin."

"They'll look for me there, too. It's not just an L.A. thing, ya know. I'm wanted in Wisconsin, Illinois, and Nevada. I'll have to change my name and what I look like."

"Didn't you already change your name once?"

"Yeah, how did you know?"

I looked at her. I stared at her. I delved deeply into her eyes and then I asked her, "Who are you?"

"Who are you?" said the Caterpillar.

"I—I hardly know, sir, just at present—at least I know who I was when I got up this morning, but I think I must have changed several times since then."

"What do you mean by that?" said the Caterpillar sternly. "Explain yourself."

"I can't explain myself, I'm afraid, sir," said Alice, "because I'm not myself you see."

"I don't see," said the Caterpillar.

"I'm afraid I can't put it more clearly." Alice replied very politely, "for I can't understand it myself to begin with; and being so many different sizes in a day is very confusing."

"It isn't," said the Caterpillar.

"Well perhaps you haven't found it out so yet," said Alice, "but when you have to turn into a chrysalis—you will some day, you know—and then after that into a butterfly, I should think you'll feel a little queer, won't you?"

"Not a bit," said the Caterpillar.

"Well perhaps your feelings may be different," said Alice, "all I know is, it would feel very queer to me."

"You!" said the Caterpillar contemptuously, "Who are you?"

Jules turned away.

"How did this whole thing with you and Bretlin start?"
"It's a long story."
"What else do we have to do?"
"Okay, if you want to know so much—"
"Yeah, I do, I do need to know."
"The less you know, the better."
I stared her down.
"A year after my mother died, I turned twenty-one and moved to Chicago. Like I told you, Louie paid for my apartment and he let me work for him if only I stayed off drugs."
"Louie was your pimp."
"Not exactly. He never made a dime off me. It was just his way of helping me out. He'd send me his business associates as favors to them. It made him look good and I kept all the money."
"He likes you."
"I guess." Yes, she did need the assurance that there were people out there who did like her and were looking out for her. "O—kay," she said and then continued with her story, "so I had my own place and was making money turning tricks. I saved my money and had over twenty grand in the bank. But then I got stupid and bored and said 'Fuck it' and started doing coke again. Now I was freebasing it. Then I began dealing, but instead of keeping the profits, I kept getting more and more addicted to it. I just kept smoking the stash I was supposed to be selling until I went broke.

"Louie admitted me into a rehab center to clean up. After I got out, I stayed with Louie—who never touched me—and stayed off drugs for three months.

"I went back to Milwaukee to look up my so-called friends, see if I could piece my life back together again somehow, ya know, back to my roots? But everybody I knew was gone, moved away, missing, in jail, in hospitals, or dead. I was lost. I tried to kill myself by swallowing nine seconals. It wasn't enough. A city sanitation worker found me in a back alley and brought me to the hospital. My stomach was pumped and I ended up in a psychiatric ward for sixty days.

"I went back to Chicago to look up Louie, but now he was

working in Vegas doing some kind of security work for one of the casinos. I was alone and back on the streets. I ended up selling myself and a giant rock of crack to an undercover officer, this detective Bretlin guy. I go to jail for five months, where I'm raped on the second night with a giant dildo by the fucking welcoming committee of my sister inmates. I got released after three months and was supposed to do all this community service and rehab shit all over again and then go back to court to prove to the judge I did all this. Well, I didn't do any of it. So now I have a bench warrant for my arrest in Illinois."

"And Bretlin?"

"I'm walking the streets again and we *bump into each other*. Well we start talking, he's asking me how I'm doing, one thing leads to another, and before you know it I'm fucking him. I'm fucking the cop who arrested me and who'd sent me to jail. I fuck him so good he starts feeding me drugs from other busts he's been on, from confiscated evidence. I had him by the balls. He knew my connection with Louie and I think he was kinda 'fraid of Louie 'cause I told him if he ever screwed me over someday I'd tell his wife and Louie. He knew his wife would just divorce him, banging a loser hooker drug addict like me, but he knew with Louie—Louie would kill him."

"How is it that you're still alive?"

"Who the fuck knows… This scumbag Bretlin is supposed to be helping people like me but he's getting me more fucked up instead. I got all kinds of restless and shit so while he was out one day I just got up and left. But I'd been planning something first. I got hold of his bank account number, forged his wife's signature on a check and withdrew seventy-five hundred from his bank. Then I split to Vegas."

"Where Louie was."

"Right. That's when Louie was just getting started in his side business exporting cars. He was moving cars from out of Vegas from Los Angeles to Mexico and Japan. He needed someone he could trust to help him steal cars. But we're not just talking Louie, we're talking close to about a hundred people involved. He also needed someone in L.A. who he could trust."

"That's why you came to L.A."

"That's why I came to L.A. Meeting up with K Dog and his boys was a major plus in my direction. K Dog was stealing cars since he was what, eleven? One of his homeboys turned a trick with Stephanie who introduced her to K Dog. She introduced me to K Dog who I introduced to Louie. K Dog had a lot of experience stealing cars. Louie needed people like him. And that helped me."

"How did it help you?"

"Because with Louie on my side I could have anything."

It was clear to me then that Jules was a product of her environment—that her constellation of acquaintances made her who she was. How could someone so indentured with a life like hers change? What heavenly intervention would allow her to lead a life of normalcy? Where was she to go next? When would she finally realize that everything she had done in her life was wrong? Did she even know right from wrong?

"So what are you going to do?" I asked her sometime again.

" 'Bout what?"

"About you?"

"Whattaya mean?"

"About getting your life together?"

"What about you? You ain't no fucking angel yourself."

❁   ❁   ❁

Jules cut her long blonde hair short and dyed it jet-black. To further change her appearance, she bought a pair of generic over-the-counter-no-prescription-needed eyeglasses to wear when she went outside.

I gave Jules a copy of my key—the copy she in fact had made. I informed the doormen in the building that "Jenny" was my "new girlfriend" and that she was staying with me until we found a place of our own. They all knew who she really was and played along. They liked Jules. She had been charming them all along. The landlord was not on premises, so at least we didn't have him to deal with.

Obviously she couldn't go into McDee's anymore in case the LAPD, DEA, or FBI went in there looking for her.

"What are you going to do?" I felt myself repeating.

"When?"

"When I'm at work. What are you going to do when I'm at work?"

"I don't know… watch TV?"

"What about your gig at the Cat's Meow?"

"I actually hadn't thought about it since the bust."

"I know you've worked there before, Peter told me. You go back to work for them they got your social security number, all that on file, right? The Feds will be looking for you in places like that."

"You're forgetting who I am, what I can do. When I worked at the Cat's Meow, I was *Trisha, Trisha Lee.*"

No, I didn't know who she was anymore.

"They're not going to check on me. All the girls working those places are running from something or someone and never give out real information. We got paid cash. There was no social security to worry about. Why? Are you worried I won't be able to share in the expenses?"

"You can't work there. But you gotta do something."

"All right, all right. I'll figure something out."

This is what she figured out: that she would get hold of K Dog, pick up a "z" on credit, and that I would deal half-grams over the bar at McDee's.

DISSOLVE TO:

It was my own fault, mostly due to Jules's sweet scented pussy and the clouds of freebasing that things had gone from bad to worse. I was no longer thinking straight. I was seeing spots in front of my eyes… the walls were moving… people were talking through the air conditioner... strange men were lurking in the halls... I was looking through the peephole every three minutes... finally I covered up the peephole and kept my ear to the door... I incessantly peeked out the window through the slats of the venetian blinds... the phone was being tapped... every sound was magnified a thousand times... opening a drawer was too loud at one o'clock in the afternoon... black velvet spiders were crawling up my arms and legs... every ten minutes I'd go into the bathroom to take a piss but couldn't... every hour I'd shit... white puss was oozing out of the inside corners of my eyes... I'd bite my fingernails until they bled... my skin was moist and clammy... I perspired all the time... I couldn't eat... I lost over twenty pounds... I chain smoked...

DOTTIE
Mickey, are you all right?

MICKEY
I'm a little under the weather that's all.

... I could not stop coughing... I was spitting up thick yellow-green-black mucous... blood was flowing out of my nose... I couldn't breathe... I watched Jules hopelessly finger her clit and try to come to orgasm to no avail for hours... every time I heard a siren on Van Nuys Boulevard they were coming for us... the TV was too loud... I couldn't turn on the stereo because no matter what the volume was it was too loud... the apartment was in total disarray... I wore the same clothes all the time... I couldn't see the floor there was so much garbage beginning to pile up... laundry needed to be done... I was afraid to go outside...

KAREN
Mickey, are you dealing drugs? I'm not going to tell Dottie, butyou know she's going to find out...

MICKEY
No, Karen, I'm not dealing drugs.

… I couldn't remember what day it was… I had no conception of time… was I supposed to work tonight or not… where was Jules? why is she taking so long? who's that knocking? who's that knocking at my door? how did you get in? how did you get past the doorman? Peter? Peter who? …

JAMIE
You don't look too good.

MICKEY
I don't feel too good.

…*now Alice, tell me the truth, did you ever eat a bat?*… you're not supposed to let him in here… K Dog isn't supposed to be in my apartment… I can't let people in the building know what's going on… I'll get evicted… …*we must burn this house down*… they're watching us… you'll get busted… I'll get busted… we'll all get busted… they're looking for me… I've got to get to work… what? it's my day off?… the phone is ringing… DON'T ANSWER IT!!!

DOTTIE
You're late for work you didn't show up for work
you're late *you're late you're late you're late for a
date* again you didn't call where were you what's
going on with you Mickey? are you all right?
Mickey? Mickey?

… who's that guy, Jules? are you fucking him? you fucking him behind my back when I'm at work? I told you nobody in this apartment… how much does he owe you? am I getting a cut? I want fifty percent… you slut… you bitch… you fucking slut bitch… how dare you…

… the walls are shaking… the WALLS are SHAKING!!!…

… somebody yell "CUT!"

Los Angeles Times… Two Strong Quakes Jolt Wide Area… 7.4 Desert Temblor Is Sharpest in Forty Years… the shock near Yucca Valley is followed by a 6.5 jolt at Big Bear Lake… a child is killed and at least three hundred fifty people are injured… rockslides block highways and a power blackout affects a half million in the region… violent temblors jostle skyscrapers as far away as Denver, rupturing the ground for forty-four miles and buckling roadways in the high desert… the terrain was self-loathing… the people were self-loathing… I was self-loathing… Hollywood was self-loathing… the place for me… a self-loathing state of mind… a self-loathing myth… I fit right in.

18

The Mustang went out of control at the intersection of Sepulveda and Victory Boulevards. I don't remember how I got there or what I was doing. I'd been up for five days without sleep. I was filled with so many different drugs and so much alcohol I was lucky to be alive. I stumbled three feet out of the totally wrecked vehicle with only a scratch on my head. I fell to the ground and blacked out. When I awoke I found myself handcuffed, slumped over on a bench in a mustard-yellow hallway of a police station.

I learned that I hadn't hurt anyone but myself when I did two three-sixties in the middle of the intersection at three fifty-six a.m., Sunday, July 5. All the traffic signals at that very moment happened to have been red. Only two automobiles with three passengers among them were waiting for the lights to change.

"Was I trying to prove something?" a police officer asked me at the Van Nuys Police Station.

Monday was an extension of the July 4th holiday weekend. Municipal personnel were short-handed due to government closings, and this included the police department and courts. I wasn't filled in with the details of the accident until Tuesday afternoon, when I was interviewed by a police sergeant, an attractive brunette female.

"Do you remember anything?" Sergeant Overland asked me, the pen in her hand poised ready to write down my statement.

"'Bout what?"

"The accident, of course."

"Oh, yeah, that…" I was a smart-ass and she didn't appreciate it. "What about my rights?" I asked.

"They were read to you when you were brought in. You don't remember, do you?" she said with tolerance. She must have interviewed hundreds of drunken-drug-addicted-assholes like me.

I shook my head.

"Do you remember the ride in the patrol car?"

I shook my head.

"Do you remember shouting obscenities after they took your photo?"

"My mug shot? I have a *mug* shot?"

"Okay, your mug shot. Do you remember the light *popping* for your mug shot?"

I shook my head.

"Mr. Collins, what do you remember?"

I thought of Jules. "Was there anybody with me?"

"No, you were alone, thank God. It's a good thing, too, because you took out the light pole on the northwest corner of the intersection with the passenger side door."

I tried to remember the accident. I didn't remember a thing. "I must have blacked out."

Overland let out a sigh and looked down at the police report lying on the table between us. "You were seen speeding recklessly out of the driveway from the Wayfarer Motel. Does that ring any bells?"

I sat there silent. It was coming back to me now. I was at the Wayfarer in a jealous rage looking for Jules because I had caught her in the act of fucking some john in my apartment after I got home early from getting out of work on a slow night, and how she left with him and somehow I ended up looking for her at the Wayfarer, and not being able to find her and all pissed off and intoxicated and sleepless I drove like a bat out of hell out into a blur of traffic not caring about anything, not caring about Jules, not caring about me, not caring about anything anymore. But I was cognizant enough by now that I knew if I had mentioned anything about Jules a.k.a. her aliases, that I'd be the one to suffer the consequences for "aiding and abetting a fugitive." So I kept my mouth shut except to say, "I'd like to talk to a public defender, please."

Bail was set at ten thousand dollars. I couldn't pay it and I refused to ask my parents for help. I told myself this is where I belong, that I would *pay the consequences*. I was in trouble. I was tired. I was tired of my life. This gave me time to get away from it. I was relieved. I needed the rest. I was giving up.

I didn't see a public defender, a Mr. Markinson, until Thursday, July 9th.

My auto insurance company would pay the destruction of city property.

I shared a comfortably spaced cell with six other men, four blacks and two Mexicans. They were cool and no one bothered anyone. We were all waiting for the next step in our processing. I kept calling my apartment collect from a pay phone located conveniently inside the jail cell but the answering machine sitting on my desk always picked up and I heard my own voice to "… please leave a message..." The operator would come on the line and then cut me off. Where was Jules? Was she purposefully not picking up the phone, monitoring all calls? Did she know it was me calling? Was she laughing at me? Was she fucking somebody at the time, is that why she wouldn't pick up the goddamn phone?

I called McDee's collect. Dottie answered. I gave her the bad news but she already knew. She scolded me as if I was her own child. I asked her if I'd have my job back when I got out. She told me that "we'll see," but I could tell by our conversation things did not look good. I had been screwing up. She knew about me and Jules, about me selling cocaine behind the bar, about me giving drinks away more than I should have, about stealing from her and how I would pretend to ring-up sales but instead take the "extra" money out of the drawer at the end of my shift. My prospect of having a job when I got out was not good, but Dottie would "think about it," maybe give me another chance, see if jail did anything to straighten me out—but who would cover my shifts?—she needed to hire someone else immediately. Charlene was not a bartender; she was a den mother, not a bartender.

I would have to come in and talk to Dottie after I got out. "Good luck, Mickey," she said to me, "take care of yourself." They were final words, final words from an ex-boss.

On Friday, July 10th, I was sentenced to thirty days in jail for my second "Driving Under the Influence" infraction and first offense for destruction of city property—both misdemeanors. The fact that I had not injured or killed anyone saved me from a felony count and years of prison. In addition, my driver's license was suspended for eighteen months, I had to complete two hundred hours of community service, and attend either Alcoholics Anonymous or Narcotics Anonymous for at least six months. I also had to attend the National Council of Alcohol and Drug Abuse three-month program to satisfy the Department of Motor Vehicles in the State of California.

Because of overcrowding, the California State penal system has what is called a "kick-out" process; and the jails were especially overcrowded due to all the arrests made during the riots. For every two days a prisoner works while incarcerated, one day is removed from his sentence. This figured out to roughly serving two-thirds of a sentence. Since I had already served five days I was looking at not twenty-five days of further incarceration, but time closer to fifteen days.

The Corrections Department's bus ride from Van Nuys Municipal Court to Los Angeles County Jail downtown in shackled wrists and ankles made me feel more like a hardened criminal than someone who was involved in a drunken automobile accident. It didn't matter, I was treated the same by the deputies.

I will never forget the first day at County. The place smelled of flatulence. I stood in a cell that must have been only sixteen-feet-by-nineteen-feet and cramped with seventy-five arrestees. We were being processed individually and slowly into California's penal computer system. Most of us were edgy and clearly neither belonged nor wanted to be there. There were others, however, who seemed relaxed, glad to see old friends, veteran criminals with their experiences of being there before and the comfort of a home. I was impatient. I wanted to hurry things along—ridiculous because I wasn't going anywhere. Nevertheless, I did have the anxious urgency to know what my cell would be like, who would be my cellmate, what job the deputies would dole out to me, whether I would get raped.

Seventy-five of us stripped, surrendered our clothes and the belongings we had in our pockets, and deposited what money we had into personal individual bank accounts. This money could be used for buying items from the jail store, such as toothpaste, gum, candy, sodas, and harmless sundries. Luckily, I had on me what I had made in tips that night, one hundred sixty-eight dollars, but it clearly was not enough, considering a smuggled pack of cigarettes cost twenty dollars.

Correction officers looked in our mouths and up our assholes for contraband. We showered all at the same time and were given two state-issued green uniforms. We were then placed in another cell awaiting each of our assigned cellblocks. Men were already selling and smoking dope. There is always a way to smuggle drugs and cigarettes into a prison—and they usually came in from other channels besides the prisoners themselves. Usually unscrupulous deputies and guards make money on the side by bringing in cigarettes and booze and heroin and pot and coke. Trustees—special appointed prisoners of good behavior—are especially privileged with connections and able to smuggle in contraband.

I was assigned to the "9000 Block" located on the top floor. This block has the fiercest reputation at County Jail—a large barrack-formation room containing hundreds of bunk beds and about two hundred criminals ranging from moving traffic violators to attempted murderers. Everyone was milling around, joking, talking on phones, yelling, poking playfully at each other, playing cards, smoking cigarettes, taking shits on open-viewed toilets, others were lying on their narrow hard-mattress bunks staring out at nothing or sleeping or trying to sleep. I surely had arrived in Hell.

No correction officer, deputy or anyone in authority told me anything about anything, if this was going to be my resting place for the next month, where, if anywhere, I would be moving to next, nothing. I assumed I would be serving my time out in this room. I found an empty bunk in the rear against the far wall. I wanted to be as far away from the activities as possible. This was all new to me and of course all the horror stories of prisoners in prisons instantly replayed themselves to me. I lay on my stomach on the top bunk facing the room. I pondered my being there and cursed repeatedly, hating myself.

❀   ❀   ❀

Beginning early the next day, names of inmates were paged over the public address system. Every few hours a group of thirty to fifty men were called out of the room and never returned. Finally, my name was called. I was being transferred out of L.A. County Jail to Saugus Jail, about sixty miles away and only a few miles past the Magic Mountain Amusement Park off I-5, on the Golden State Freeway. Saugus is a minimum security prison where most misdemeanor convicts serve their time—usually no longer than twelve months. Those incarcerated included mostly petty thieves, larcenies, looters from the now infamous riots, assaults and batteries, drunken drivers, and traffic violators. A few miles up the hill where the maximum security prison is located the felons serve their sentences from one to twenty years to life. That's where the hard-core are kept: the armed robbers, rapists, attempted murderers, and murderers.

Saugus is like boot camp, with rows of aluminum barracks spread out one after another. There's a baseball field, basketball court, and workout weight area for those inclined to stay fit. An all-denominational chapel is situated in the middle of the grounds. The mess hall is one of the first buildings near the entrance/exit of the camp.

My crib was in A-7, the last house at the very end of the camp up a hill near the laundry building where eventually I would be working. A-7 is again, one large barrack-style room. Fifty double bunks, one hundred prisoners. A-7 has air-conditioning, color cable television, open toilets and sinks. The room was surprisingly clean except for the odor of men. I was assigned an empty top bunk and immediately became friends with a top bunk neighbor next to me, "Snake Eyes," a black inmate from Compton who was there after being picked up on a warrant charge. I didn't ask what the warrant was for. You learn not to ask too many questions while in jail, and Snake Eyes didn't volunteer why he was there. We hung with each other and formed a close friendship. We were released on the same day. I gave him a call a few days later and learned from his sister that "Robert" had just been killed by a Crip bullet.

It took me three days to acclimate, not wake up from night sweats, to feel comfortable and at home while being confined in a prison. I was assigned to work laundry duty for two four-hour shifts six days a week. We washed prisoners' uniforms from all over Southern California. The laundry machines were eight feet high and sounded like jet engines. Jules would have no trouble climbing inside the oversized dryers.

The topic of conversation between inmates was always who was getting kicked out and when. A chart was posted outside the mess hall explaining how the kick out process worked, and an inmate could actually figure out when he was going to be released. With uncanny accuracy I saw men predict exactly to the day when they were going to be released. I figured my kick-out time to fourteen days.

I exercised, played softball, lifted weights, relaxed, slept a lot. After a week I felt healthy. My head was clear. I quit smoking.

I started going to the chapel. Some days I would just go in and get on my knees and pray for hours for God to forgive me, to help me, to help me find myself, and to get out of the mess I was in. I prayed for redemption, for God to listen to me and to answer my prayers, to tell me why I was the way I was, why I committed so many sins. I prayed for a miracle to change my ways, to change the way I felt about myself and the world around me, to change my behavior, to change the hate I had toward myself, to stop being an addict.

Peter came to visit. Jules couldn't visit because she was a wanted criminal. Identification needs to be shown when visiting someone in a prison.

"What's going on?"

"She's tearing your place apart."

"What she doing?"

"What do you think?"

"Get her out of there."

"How? How am I going to get *her out* of *your* apartment? She can't live with me. I live with my dad, you think he's going to allow her bullshit to go on? He hates *me*, man."

"I don't care where she goes, just get her out of there."

Peter shook his head like it was an impossible feat.

"Are you staying at my place? Are you fucking Jules while I'm in jail?" I asked him.

"Man, you know I never fucked her and never will. Blow jobs, yeah, sure, but I won't stick my dick into her like you are."

We both paused to think.

"She's got everyone by the balls," Peter 'fessed up.

"What do you mean?"

"She's fucking a doorman, K Dog is always up there, there's traffic in and out…"

I held my head in my hands. "Fuck."

"You did this to yourself, man."

"I know."

"She's living rent free. You think she's gonna send a check to your landlord, keep things all tidy and nice for you for when you get out? Clean the windows? I told you a long time ago to get rid of her."

"All right, all right. Just do me a favor, don't let her get me thrown out of there. She'll listen to you. Do what you can."

"She doesn't listen to anybody, man. I don't know what you want me to do."

"How about being my friend and helping me out for once. How about that?"

19

Freedom. Everyone should spend at least one week in jail to realize what freedom is and how it is to be cherished and not taken for granted.

The worst day of my life was being inducted into the hall of degenerate fame of Los Angeles County Jail; the best day of my life was getting released; but it was a tormenting process of waiting day by day, hour by hour, minute by minute, and second by excruciating second to regain my freedom.

Just as time was a factor in my release, so was space. From my final holding cell at County to where the T-shirt, Levis, and boots I was arrested in were returned to me, to the open door of freedom, were yards, feet, and inches before I was allowed to reenter the open air of a new life, of a new chance, a new dance.

Twenty-six of us new-born ex-inmates sat in a drab-green room wearing the clothes we came in with and waited as each of our names were called one by one by a deputy. Men responded quickly to their names by jumping out of their seats and scampering, escorted by a second deputy, into a closed-door room.

My name was called and I bolted up out of my seat. The next room was actually a short hallway. In front of me, a three-inch thick steel door stood between me and the "first day of the rest of my life." On my left behind a glassed cutout in a wall sat an African-American female clerk at a computer, her nametag read, "Freeman."

Freeman said my name, told me what my birth date and social security number were, and asked, "Is this correct?"

"Yes, ma'am."

She was checking the computer to see if there were any outstanding warrants for my arrest. I heard stories of inmates only seconds away from being released, merely three feet from THE DOOR, only to be immediately returned to the patience of confinement because a new warrant for their arrest appeared in the computer for a past crime they had committed, and the record had only recently entered the California penal system's computer during the interim of their stay at Hotel California.

Freeman's frozen face stared into the computer screen. She pecked at the computer's keyboard slowly and patiently. She was probably thinking about what she was going to cook for dinner for her kids that night. My hands perspired. I felt clammy. I knew I had no other warrants for my arrest, but what if there was a mistake? What if she entered just one wrong number, what if there were glitches in the system and I was to serve another nineteen days behind bars, or my file had somehow been merged with another Michael Collins, a Michael Collins who butchered his wife and kids and was to spend a lifetime incarcerated, and she didn't believe who I really was, she didn't want to re-punch my numbers. *No ma'am, that's the wrong Michael Collins you have there. Surely there's a mistake. I'll just leave right now and you'll never have to see me again.*

Without saying a word, Freeman reached for a manila envelope and handed it to me through a small opening in the glass. The envelope contained my belongings: a set of keys (including two car keys that were now useless), my wallet, and a small white envelope containing the remaining money I practically had left in the world: nine dollars.

A loud buzzer sounded. It came from the direction of the heavy metal door. I walked towards it, turned the aluminum door handle clockwise, and pushed the door forward. It opened. I walked out into a bright afternoon sunlight. No one stopped me. I allowed the door to slam behind me.

I was eager to start my life over again.

I walked. I took out my ATM card at a Bank of America. From what I remembered I should have had about four hundred fifty dollars in the bank. My balance read, "No available funds." Okay, maybe in a fit of drugged ecstasy I withdrew more money than I should have and didn't remember—but I always kept the receipts and my wallet did not contain any.

After taking a transfer of three buses it took me two hours to get home (an eighteen-minute car ride with little traffic on the Hollywood Freeway).

The doorman greeted me with consternation.

I knocked on my own apartment door. If Jules was there I didn't want to scare her by just walking in and getting shot. There was no answer. I put my ear to the door and didn't hear anything. I cautiously entered my apartment not knowing what to expect. The place was a mess. Cigarette ashes overfilled ashtrays, empty beer cans and liquor bottles told me that a party had been going on there since the time I was arrested.

I called out Jules's name and got no response. I walked into the bedroom. The room was trashed. My bed looked as if it had not been made since the last time I slept in it. Wine stains, cum stains, and cigarette burns decorated the sheets. Pillows were on the floor and Jules's sexually perverse clothes were scattered everywhere.

I went back into the living area and vowed to throw Jules out as soon as she walked through the door.

The LED light on my answering machine was blinking furiously: There were twenty-nine messages—mostly hang-ups and K-Dog going "Yo, it's me, pick up." My mom called asking how I was doing, they hadn't heard from me in a long, long time. My brother called to say he was stopping in Los Angeles on business for two days on his way back from Tokyo to New York and if we could get together he'd like to take me out to dinner.

Messages to call my landlord, and then this: "Mr. Collins, again your rent is overdue. I have not heard from you, but that's the least of your problems. I've been getting a lot of calls from your neighbors and it seems that you've been having a lot of loud parties and you've got people coming and going at all hours of the night. I've left several messages and have not heard from you. I have no choice but to ask you to remove yourself and your belongings from the premises by the end of this month. You've got a girl staying with you, Jenny I think her name is, she needs to be out immediately."

Another message from my brother saying that he was now in L.A., and to call him at the Premiere Hotel, where he was staying for the next two nights. Another message from my brother this time telling me that he called McDee's and found out that I was in jail and that he had to leave on a flight that day and that he was calling Mom and Dad to ask them if they knew anything about my car accident and getting arrested.

A call from Dad.

I opened the drawer where I kept my checkbook. It was gone. Jules must have forged a check and withdrew the remaining money I had in the bank.

I was broke.

I plumped myself down on the sofa and couldn't move off of it. My world had fallen apart.

I prayed to God and asked what to do next.

Night came and I heard no answer.

I sat in darkness.

The phone rang, startling me out of a feverish sleep. I didn't answer it. I heard my own recorded voice "…to leave a message…" Click. A hang-up. I felt a sick feeling in my stomach and my brain felt on fire.

These were my options: talk to my parents, tell them the half-truth and ask for money; call the landlord and lie to him that I was in New York because of a family emergency and that I would kick "Jenny" out and promise to pay the rent on time if he would just give me another chance even though I already owe him for one month and had no way of getting him next month's rent in one week; search the apartment for a gun that maybe Jules had hidden and go out and pull an armed robbery; scrape together enough money to purchase a large amount of cocaine, cut it and resell it in half-grams until I was able to make enough money to get back on my feet again; go out first thing in the morning and find another bartending job where I can immediately make cash tips; ask either Peter, Gary, Craig, or Ed, if I could stay with them until I got a job and back on my feet again; get arrested for killing Jules for getting me in this mess so I could go back to jail and have a place to sleep and eat and work at a forever-prison-issued-job and not have to worry about anything for the rest of my cursed life; walk outside into the stream of Van Nuys Boulevard traffic, get hit by a car or bus or truck, land in the hospital so I could buy more time—or the grave so I could buy *all* time; just hang myself right then and there; plead with Dottie to get my job back, fall into the same old habits and get arrested all over again; join the Peace Corps; put my thumb out at the entrance ramp to the 101 Ventura Freeway North and see where it takes me and what each day will bring; jump out the window; slam my head against the wall; drink rat poison; fill the bathtub with warm water, step in and slash my wrists; stab a knife in my heart; inject myself with Windex; trade my television set in for one good bag of heroin and O.D.; talk to a priest; walk into the L.A. Free Medical Clinic and have a nervous breakdown; ignore the landlord's request and stay there as long as I could; just leave Los Angeles.

The phone rang again. "…leave a message…"

"Yo, it's me, pick up."

It was K Dog's voice. I picked up the phone.

"K Dog, its Mickey."

"When you get out?"

"Yesterday."

"Cool."

"You looking for Jules?"

"She there?"

"No. When was the last time you saw her?"

"I ain't seen her in a week. Talked to her couple days ago, said she needed somethin' would call me back… never did."

"Listen, K Dog, I need to see you."

" 'Bout what?"

"Not over the phone."

"It like that?"

"Can you come up my way?"

"Ain't got no car, huh."

"I totaled it."

"I heard. You lucky to be alive."

"I know. And a lot of shit goin' down here, too."

There was a long silence on the other end, then, "Meet me on the corner of Van Nuys and Burbank. I ain't gettin' near your crib. Too hot. We'll take a ride. You know my car. See you in an hour," K Dog said and hung up.

Burbank Boulevard was a ten-minute walk up Van Nuys Boulevard.

❁   ❁   ❁

Two hours later K Dog picked me up in his Beamer. "Jump" by Kris Kross was blasting out from a CD. K-Dog had come stompin'. He had somethin' pumpin' to keep me jumpin'. We drove east on Burbank Boulevard.

K Dog lowered the volume on the music. "Spent some time with the homeboys, eh? Where they hole you up at?"

"County first, then Saugus."

"Shit, Saugus ain't nothin.' That like kindergarten. You lucky you didn't stay at County, you would o' been all fucked up by now, 'specially if you in thirty-eight hundred."

"What's thirty-eight hundred?"

"Crip module."

I didn't respond.

"What you want to see K Dog 'bout?"

"A favor."

"Go on."

"Lost my bartending job—"

"That lady boss fire your ass, huh?"

190

"Red hot fired. I got no job, no car, I think Jules forged some checks of mine…"

"Ain't that a surprise."

"She fucked me over with my living situation, soon no place to live."

"You want me to kill the bitch?"

"No."

"How much you need then?"

"I don't want to have to borrow money from you. If you can credit me an eight ball, I can push it, re-up with you and when I get a couple grand together we call it quits. I move out of my place, I get away from Jules, and you and I never see each other again. I can't be doin' this. I need to change my life."

"Yeah, jail got to you, all right. Where you plan on pushing it, that place you used to work at?"

"No. Universal Bar and Grill."

"Where's that?"

"Studio City, across from Universal Studios."

"You know people there?"

"Yeah, I know lots of people there looking for powder. A lot of movie tech people do coke and they got money. Today's Friday, if you can front me an eight ball, I'll have it sold tonight, then I can re-up for tomorrow night."

"Tell you what K Dog's gonna do. K Dog's gonna give you an eight ball on credit. Just do yourself a favor. Don't smoke it. You won't be able to stop. You'll fuck yourself up. You'll smoke the whole fucking thing and then you'll owe K Dog lots o' money and he'll come after you with you wishing you were back in jail."

K Dog reached under the dashboard and pulled out a handful of eight balls. "Here, pick one."

I picked one with clumps of hard powder and put it in my pocket. "Thanks."

"You still know my pager number?" K Dog asked me.

I recited K Dog's pager number.

"Call me when you ready to re-up." He then reached under the dash again and pulled out a .22 pistol. "Stole this from the bitch a while back, she blamed it on The Saint, but I the one who took it. You take it."

"I don't want it."

"I'm given' you the gat for your own protection."

"No."

"Why not?"

"Because the first person I'd use it on is me and I don't want that temptation."

K Dog put the gun back under the dashboard.

That night I took a bus down Ventura Boulevard to the Universal Bar and Grill. I sold half-grams and grams out of the eight ball, then took a cab back to my place. On Saturday I gave what I owed to K Dog. I was clear of owing him any money. I had cash on hand and another eight ball.

I decided to celebrate my being out of jail, my new-found freedom, and the fact that maybe I could get back on my feet and sustain myself by way of selling cocaine. I cooked up a half-gram and smoked it. I cooked up a gram and smoked that. I cooked up another gram and smoked that... and... and... and... In six hours I had smoked the entire eight ball and realized that I couldn't go through with the idea of being a drug dealer.

I wanted to find Jules and get the money she stole from me, not only because I obviously needed the money, but also because I didn't want her to think she had it over on me.

Sunday afternoon I walked into McDee's for the first time since I was released from jail. Dottie always took Sundays off and I knew it wouldn't be busy. I didn't want to see too many people and answer questions. But I knew Charlene would be there and she would know where Jules was.

"I don't know where she is. Haven't seen her since you went to jail. FBI was in here looking for her, though," Charlene informed me.

"What she do?"

"They ask about me?"

"They asked who she hung around with. I told them I really didn't know her that well. But Dottie was here, she told them all about the car being stolen last year out of the parking lot. They talked to Jamie, too; all she said was that Jules just came in here a few times. They looked around and left."

"Did they talk to Peter?"

"Peter wasn't here. He doesn't know where she is, either. You're in trouble, huh."

"I think so."

Charlene shook her head, "Better lay low."

"Landlord wants me out, too."

"Shit, Mickey, what are you gonna do?" Charlene asked, genuinely concerned.

"I don't know." I stood there motionless, perplexed. "I don't want to be in this movie anymore."

20

Monday morning I called my landlord asking him if I can pay back the money I owed him from July and that I was working on getting the rent together for August and that my *ex*-girlfriend was already gone. He told me he wanted me out. He told me he didn't care about the rent anymore and that I was trouble and he just wanted me "vacant from the premises." I apologized for all the trouble I gave him and he said, "We all make mistakes."

Again I sat depressed with new options of what to do next running through my mind.

The phone rang, awakening me out of my self-pitied daze. It was Charlene. "You see the *Times* today?"

"No, why?"

"Jules got arrested. Big bust at the Wayfarer."

"What happened?"

"They raided the place Saturday night. Knocked down doors, broke into rooms, Jules was there... place was crawling with Feds."

"No shit."

"Yeah," I heard Charlene chuckle and inhale a drag off a cigarette, "big story."

"What are you talking about?"

" A regular drug factory. Jules, too. I didn't know she did all that stuff."

"What stuff?"

"Attempted murder. Did you know about that?"

I didn't say anything. My silence answered her question.

"Maybe you should get out of your apartment now, go someplace out of L.A. They might be looking for you. Who knows what she's going to say."

There was silence on both ends of the phone as we absorbed the revelation of new events.

"Go get the paper, then call me back," Charlene said.

"I'm going to need a place to stay."

"I wish I could help you; my place is like sleepover camp I got so many people crashing over here. Gary stayed last night, he got really drunk, we played cards all night—"

"Let me go get the paper."

"Call me back."

Los Angeles Times, Monday, July 27, 1992
Feds Storm Van Nuys Motel
Story by
Maggie Russell
Associated Press

With the sound of chopper blades and Los Angeles Police Department helicopters beaming powerful search lights from five hundred feet overhead, Federal Bureau of Investigation agents and Drug Enforcement Administration agents with guns drawn invaded and raided the Wayfarer Motel on Sepulveda Boulevard in Van Nuys, California, late Saturday night in a Federal, State, and City drug, prostitution, and illegal alien search and seizure.

Authorities from the three law enforcement sectors had been monitoring the activities of the motel for six months in what Lieutenant Larry Mullens of the LAPD described, "a motel den of iniquity," where illegal female aliens from Japan were living virtually rent free in order to provide services of prostitution to Asian businessmen visiting Los Angeles. One of the owners of the motel, Sami Yamaguchi, 59, who has criminal ties to the Yakuza—the Japanese mafia, was apprehended. American women were also involved in the scheme to lure both Asian and American men to the motel for the provision of sex and drugs.

"We think a lot of what has gone on here," Agent Donald J. Barrows, the leading investigator of the FBI said, "has to do with a Nevada corporation. We can't exactly say right now who we're looking at in Nevada. It's a complicated paper matter of who actually owns the motel, but our sources think it's not wholly a Japanese-run outfit, but domestically owned as a shell corporation going through many different hands," Barrows further offered.

The 56-room Wayfarer was also a factory for the making of the new popular drug "ecstasy"—methylenedioxymethamphetamine— or MDMA, and a mid-shipping point of fentanyl citrate—"China White"— heroin imported from Asia. DEA agents discovered a series of three rooms joined together where Asian women in surgical masks were working at long tables manufacturing and packaging large quantities of ecstasy and cut heroin. "All together we found over 500 kilograms of heroin, 200 kilograms of cocaine, 100 kilograms of ecstasy-making ingredients and about 50 kilograms of marijuana throughout the motel," agent Sinclair "Sonny" Simms of the DEA said. "This is a nice haul."

Many of the American women at the motel have past criminal records, warrants for their arrest, or are either on probation or parole from a prison sentence. "We were especially pleased when some of the women and men we apprehended were wanted by either the FBI or LAPD," Simms added.

One particular woman the LAPD had been looking for in the last three months and the FBI for two, is Joanne Luchenski, 28, of Milwaukee, Wisconsin. Luchenski has been running from the law all her life and is considered by the FBI as a career offender with a criminal livelihood. "Someone who leads a 'criminal livelihood' is someone who has a 'pattern' of criminal conduct," Barrows explained. "It means they plan criminal acts occurring over a substantial period of time. These acts may involve a single cause of conduct or independent offenses. It means that Luchenski derived her income from the pattern of criminal conduct in a twelve-month period and that the totality of circumstances shows that such criminal conduct was her primary occupation in that twelve-month period."

Luchenski is being charged with numerous crimes, including fraud and related activity in connection with identification documents; deceit and forgery; racketeering as it relates to interstate transportation of stolen property and interstate transportation of stolen motor vehicles; aggravated assault with a deadly weapon; assault with intent to commit murder; larceny; prostitution; property damage or destruction; burglary of a residence or a structure other than a residence; armed robbery; extortion by force or threat of injury or serious damage; unlawful possession of a controlled substance; and finally, violation of parole.

I finished reading the article, which went on further about Yamaguchi's past history, how he came to America 'the land of opportunity' with the intent to become rich through other people's passions.

I paced the apartment, studying the contents of my possessions. What did I really need? What could I live without? What could I leave behind? The landlord wants me out, so I'll get out. I'll get out now and take only what I need.

I called Charlene back and told her what I was doing.

She came over that afternoon with Peter and her Dodge Charger. The car was big and clunky and had a lot of room. They both helped me move my personal belongings into a storage unit in North Hollywood under Charlene's name. Large items like furniture, we just moved down to the outside dumpster at the rear of the building. Someone would pick it up.

I thanked Charlene and kissed her good-bye. She gave me a few dollars. I told Peter to go fuck himself. And with one over-the-shoulder bag and one hand-carry tote bag containing my scripts, I walked. I didn't know to where. But I was free. I was still clear and free and all I thought about was how far away I wanted to be from Jules, from McDee's, from Charlene, from Peter, from Jamie, from K Dog, from Ed, Harold, and Craig, from the movie business, from the smog, from the eucalyptus trees, the date palms and hibiscus plants, from Hollywood, from Los Angeles, from the State of California.

21

New York City is not a bad place. I've been living here for a number of years now and doing a lot of writing. When I first moved back East I made my living by working as a bartender. The restaurant I worked at was Café Phoebe on the Upper East Side. Jackets and ties are required for the men, it's that kind of a place. The *New York Times* gave it four stars. I didn't date the women I met there.

Tim was the one who bailed me out of California. After I strolled the streets of Los Angeles aimlessly with baggage in hand for two days figuring out what to do, where to go, wondering how was I going to live, I finally succumbed to my misfortunes and called my brother in Manhattan. After I hung up with him I walked sixteen miles to LAX. A ticket, purchased by my brother, was waiting for me at American Airlines. The flight was for the next day. I sat the entire time in a daze and contemplated my failures. I had arrived in the land of dreams with further dreams and hopes of success. Instead, I was leaving as a failure, broke, despondent, suicidal. At least I had my family who never stopped loving me, who didn't know the whole story, the truth—till now.

My DUI infraction case was transferred to the New York Courts. I completed all the necessary requirements, including the two hundred hours of community service, the National Council of Alcohol and Drug Abuse three-month program, and the required six months of AA or Narcotics Anonymous meetings. I'd be lying if I said I've been clean and sober since. I've had a few "relapses" as they say in the parlance of drug culture; however, I still attend AA meetings every day and have been clean and sober as of this writing. I can hear the music again.

I've completed eight screenplays and twenty-four short stories. This is my first novel.

I re-enrolled at New York University, but instead of completing my studies in the filmmaking program, I opted to concentrate in the writing curriculum. I've earned my Masters Degree in English Literature.

Over the course of the last decade I've kept in touch with Charlene, to whom I gave permission to do what she wanted with my stored possessions. She had mailed a few personal belongings to me and threw away mostly everything else. Every once in a while we talk by telephone and she fills me in with the latest gossip, what is what and who is doing what to whom.

Two weeks after I disappeared from Los Angeles, Peter was arrested for selling an ounce of marijuana to a high school student fifteen hundred feet from North Hollywood High School, punishable with a fine of ten thousand dollars and/or two years in jail. It was Peter's first offense. He had no money, his father wouldn't give him any, so he paid the price by taking the time in jail and served *two weeks*. He was back at McDee's like time hadn't changed a thing.

Bones's lawyer kept continuances on court dates but time finally caught up with Bones and he was sentenced to serve five years in prison. He served three. No one has seen him since.

Bill served four years in prison. After his release, and according to parole requirements, Bill attended numerous drug rehabilitation programs. He moved back to Oakland, California, reunited with his mom and dad and has been clean ever since. No one ever heard from Stephanie again.

K Dog was killed by a Blood. However, witnesses say that a Cadillac with Nevada license plates was seen on the block at the time K Dog was shot down.

Louie Vicente was extradited to Chicago and was charged by the United States Justice Department in Superior Court with a total of one hundred sixty-six counts of federal crimes, including racketeering; interstate transportation of stolen motor vehicles; interstate transportation of stolen property; fraud and other related activities in connection with identification documents; obstruction of justice; bribery; sports bribery; extortionate credit transactions; aggravated assault; attempted murder; conspiracy or solicitation to commit murder; murder; larceny; embezzlement; international transferring and transportation of stolen vehicles; extortion by force or threat of injury or serious damage; altering or removing motor vehicle identification numbers, or trafficking in motor vehicles or parts with altered or obliterated identification numbers; laundering of monetary transactions in property derived from specified unlawful activities; continuing criminal enterprises; forgery, obstructing or impeding the administration of justice; bribery of public officials and witnesses; conspiracy to commit several offenses, duplicity, indictment or information; smuggling, transporting, or harboring unlawful aliens; collection of extensions of credit by extortionary means; fraud and false statements in a court of law; perjury; transmission of wagering information; misuse of evidence of citizenship or naturalization; fraud and misuse of visas, permits, and other documents; interstate and foreign travel or transportation in aid of racketeering enterprises; and violent crimes in aid of racketeering activities. He was acquitted of most charges, sentenced to twenty years and is up for his first parole review any time now.

Jamie met a divorced yet successful real estate agent. He asked Jamie to marry him. Jamie said yes and she and Ashley are living with him and his two young boys in Tarzana, California. Jamie has a part-time job working as a cashier at Sav-On in Sherman Oaks, down the street from where I once lived and where Jules, K-Dog, and Bill would occasionally steal a car out of the parking lot.

Harold died of diabetes complications.

Ed's wife divorced him after filing a restraining order against him for his continual beatings on her.

Craig got fired from Pacific Gas & Electric for drinking on the job.

Gary took a spill on his Harley and has brain damage. He's a quadriplegic who lives in a wheelchair and drools.

Dottie moved back to New Jersey to take care of her father, who was afflicted with Alzeimher's disease. Dottie sold the bar to Charlene.

Charlene didn't change a thing after purchasing "McDee's Cocktail Lounge & Bar," keeping the name and the sign outdoors on Victory Boulevard that read, "Coldest Beer in the Valley." Charlene still sits at the end of the bar, reads the *Los Angeles Times*, and fills in every box of the crossword puzzle. She no longer sells drugs and won't tolerate anyone who does. Business has gone down.

Jules received a sentence of nine years. She probably did seven of them and is out by now—unless she's back in for something else. No one has heard from or seen her since. I sometimes think about the time she stumbled out of McDee's drunk and high and striking poses to "Vogue" and promised us all that she would be back. Who knows where she could be, she could be in another institution somewhere, prison again, or dead. Far as I'm concerned she's just a bad memory.

What was it that Bogart said to Ingrid Bergman in *Casablanca*? "Of all the gin joints, in all the towns, in all the world, she walks into mine."

Now, she's forever gone and out of my life.

Thank God.

FADE OUT.

Printed in the United States
20099LVS00002B/163

9 781413 725636